THE ONE WHO

Changed Everything

SECOND CHANCE FIRE STATION
Book Five

TARA GRACE
ERICSON

Edited by Editing Done Write
Cover Design: Jess Mastorakos
Cover Photo: O'Ryan Empire
Los Angeles, CA
Cover Models: Jeff Poster and Shirley Poster

Paperback ISBN-13: 978-1-949896-73-2
Ebook ISBN-13: 978-1-949896-74-9

To my boys.
You three changed everything. And I wouldn't change anything.

"For I, the LORD, do not change."

MALACHI 3:6

Contents

CHAPTER 1

Samantha

The piercing wail of the fire alarm sliced through the hush of the Minden Public Library, and I jumped out of my chair. Heart thudding with unwelcome memories of the past, I kept my voice even, masking my concern with a steady calm as I directed the few patrons here on a weekday morning toward the exits. As chaos threatened to bubble up inside me, I caught sight of Daniel, my weekday volunteer, sheepishly waving away smoke from the staff break room.

A sigh of relief accompanied my automatic eye roll.

"Daniel, what did you do this time?" I chided lightly, hoping humor would keep the panic at bay for everyone present.

"Sorry, Ms. Brown. I guess multitasking isn't my strong suit," he replied, his face flushed with embarrassment. He was young, barely out of high school, but a sweet kid. Clueless, but sweet.

"Let's focus on getting everyone out safely. We'll work on your cooking skills later," I said with a gentle smile despite the tightness in my chest.

Though it seemed there was no real danger, I made the rounds, scanning for any stragglers, my sensible shoes silent on the well-worn carpet. The acrid smell of burnt plastic clawed at my nostrils, covering the usual scent of aged paper and polished wood that comforted me on quieter days. I couldn't help but think of the nightclub fire—a night that altered my entire life—and those thoughts added speed to my steps. As though I could outrun the memories.

"Anyone here?" I called out, peeking between the stacks, ensuring no one was left behind. I was pretty sure no one was upstairs in the reference section or community rooms, but I did a quick check just to be sure.

Once outside, I let the fresh air fill my lungs, a welcome change from the smoky tendrils that had chased us from the library. My eyes, stinging slightly from the irritation, swept over the small cluster of folks huddled on the sidewalk, their faces etched with concern and curiosity. A few elderly gentlemen, a mom with two young kids, and a middle-aged woman still clutching the romance novel she'd been about to check out stood like misplaced characters, plucked from different stories and genres, all sharing this unexpected plot twist.

The wail of sirens crescendoed then stopped as a gleaming red fire truck rolled to a halt in front of us. My heart, which had been thrumming steadily from the adrenaline of the evacuation, skipped a beat—not because of the so-called emergency, but at the sight of the man in the passenger seat of the truck.

Could this morning get any worse?

I hadn't seen that face since the Spring Sparks Auction, and I'd done everything in my power to make sure he hadn't seen me then. I'd harbored a secret hope—a foolish one—that I might somehow continue to avoid him. The man didn't belong here anyway. But in a town the size of Minden, avoidance was never truly an option.

As for before the Spring Sparks Auction? It had been fourteen years since I laid eyes on his cool green eyes and dimpled chin. And I'd hoped it would be even longer.

I slid behind Daniel's bulky frame, ducking my

head to stay out of sight. But I couldn't help stealing a peek. I was just a girl, after all. And the most gorgeous man I'd ever met was here.

Evan Mercer stepped out of the firetruck, his tall frame clad in turnout gear that marked him unmistakable against the backdrop of the fire truck's vibrant hue. He moved with an assuredness that spoke volumes of his experience, assessing the situation with the precision of someone born to handle crises, despite the fact I knew he'd been born with a silver spoon and no doubt a nanny or five to care for his every need.

His focus was absolute, and his eyes moved toward our small group. For a suspended moment, time seemed to slow—just as it did when we were younger, before life quickly taught me the cost of our recklessness. His eyes held a depth I didn't remember, swirling with emotion that didn't match the practicality of his movements as his gaze slid past me, still seeking their target. A breath shuddered out of me in relief.

Maybe I was being paranoid. What were the odds he even remembered me? That week in Florida had involved more than a few drinks and a severe lack of sleep.

I watched, still half hiding behind the shifting

group of evacuees, as he barked orders to his team, clearly outlining the steps they would take next. He glanced around, his eyes landing on the small group of bystanders gathered on the sidewalk. "Who's in charge here?"

My heart plummeted into my stomach. Maybe lower. Yeah, it was all the way to my toes. I was going to have to grab a spatula to peel it off the side-walk from the way it had crashed at the realization that I couldn't hide any more. Mr. Henley was off today, which meant I was the most senior library employee.

I swallowed and stepped forward, relinquishing the cover my volunteer had been unknowingly providing. "That would be me."

His eyes widened. "Sam?"

So much for not remembering me. Had he really not known I lived here? The shock in his voice was genuine, I could tell that much. I couldn't dwell on it though. His hand reached up, as though he were going to touch me.

I stepped back, putting space between us that I desperately needed. "I walked through the whole building," I said, keeping my voice calm and profes-sional. Surely, he couldn't hear the way my throat was tightening. "Everyone is out. I'm pretty sure it is just a microwave ramen tragedy, courtesy of a volunteer." I could barely hear my own words over the clamor of my racing heart. My jaw set firm even as my emotions threatened to spill over like ink on pristine pages.

Evan's hand stilled on its way toward me and his brow furrowed. He cleared his throat, his eyes, full of questions, tracing my features. "We'll do a sweep of the space and give you the all clear."

Anger swelled within me, rising like the tide against the levees of my self-control. Betrayal, sharp and bitter, clawed its way up my throat. What right did he have to have questions? He was the one who never called. The one who'd disappeared after our week together and our one-night indiscretion. The night that resulted in a daughter he'd never met.

Though the storm of emotions threatened to drown me, I kept my expression carefully unreadable. I wouldn't let him shake me.

"Thank you."

His frown deepened. "Sam?"

I steeled myself internally, clenching my fists tight enough to feel my nails bite into the flesh of my palms. This was a test of everything I'd built, every wall I'd erected around my heart fourteen years ago.

Today, I wouldn't let them crumble—not in front of Evan Mercer, not in front of anyone.

"We really appreciate the quick response from Minden's finest. I'll be over here with my staff waiting for the all clear."

It was everything I could do to deliver the detached lines without tipping my hand.

He nodded slowly, an acknowledgment weighted with a history I'd prefer remained buried in the ashes of our past. His gaze lingered on mine, searching for a crack in my armor, a hint of the warmth that had long since turned cold. "I'll come find you," he said.

The words were right, the tone professional—yet something in me twisted. I knew–and he knew– what he was saying with those words. I nodded back, a curt motion that put a period at the end of a sentence I wished I could erase.

The moment Evan turned away, his focus shifting to the men awaiting his command, my eyes betrayed me. They traced the familiar line of his jaw, the set of his shoulders as they squared against the uncertainty of danger. A cocktail of resentment mingled with an aching sense of something lost, something I couldn't quite grasp or name, stirred in my chest. I wrenched my gaze away, fearing he might glance back and catch the unguarded tremor of vulnerability I fought so hard to conceal.

I watched from the periphery as Evan directed his team. It struck me then how unexpected life could be. That Evan Mercer, with the weight of the Mercer family's expectations looming over him like the sprawling Chicago estate they owned, would choose to race into fires instead of basking in the glow of society pages.

And that he would end up here of all places.

The last time we spoke, it was all whispered promises wrapped around us like bedsheets, commitments for forever together spilling recklessly between us.

Promises that smoldered into ash when reality came crashing down.

He never called. And when I realized exactly who he was? I stopped hoping he would and started praying that he'd forget about me entirely.

A part of me still couldn't reconcile this man, clad in turnout gear, with the Evan whose laughter chased me on the beach, whose dreams seemed so distant from the heroics he embodied now. Yet there he was, the boy with summer-kissed hair turned man with a shield of bravery. A man who could take everything from me in an instant if he knew.

"Sam?" Daniel's voice, sharp with concern, cut through the fog of my musings, yanking me back from the brink of memory's chasm. I jerked my head up, blinking away the remnants of a past.

"Right here," I replied, more to myself than to him. "What's next?"

"Alright, everyone, the situation is under control," I announced to the small cluster of faces, their eyes reflecting the flickering lights of the firetruck. "Thank you for your patience."

"Is it safe?"

"Completely safe, Mr. Jenkins," I reassured him with a smile. "You'll be back to your chess game in no time."

"I was losing anyway," he grumbled with a glance at Mr. Ross standing next to him. The two elderly men had been playing chess at the library every weekday morning since I had started working there eight years ago.

Another firefighter told me we had the all clear, much to my relief. Back inside, the library was silent, as if holding its breath. The same way it greeted me each morning when I unlocked the doors.

I stepped over the threshold, the familiar scent of bound paper tainted with the acrid smell of burnt plastic. It had been here, in these aisles, that I became

Samantha Brown, the librarian. The warrior single mother determined to build a better life for her daughter. I knew my daughter deserved better than the peeling, dirty linoleum floors of the ramshackle single-wide I had grown up in, with empty beer bottles piled in the corners and empty shelves in the fridge.

I wasn't the Samantha Brown who, for a blink of a week, dared to dream that love could bridge the gaps between two very different worlds.

Evan Mercer. The name etched itself into my thoughts with the persistence of a watermark on important documents—visible under certain light, impossible to ignore once seen. Evan Mercer had officially invaded my world once again. Last time, he'd won me over so quickly. But back then, I'd had no reason to keep him out.

Now, I had to. He could take everything. One word from a judge that the Mercer family was petitioning for custody and Sophia would be ripped from my arms. We weren't in Chicago, but we certainly weren't far enough away. Maybe I should have moved when I'd had the chance years ago. But I wouldn't have guessed Evan would come here–not in a million years. What had happened in the last fourteen years to lead him here?

I shoved that curiosity down. It didn't matter. Couldn't matter.

Why he was here was irrelevant. He hadn't cared to find me in all the years since our spring break fling in Florida, and he wouldn't care now. I just needed to make sure he didn't find out about Sophia. I couldn't be sure he would want her. But if he did? I'd never forgive myself if I lost her.

My daughter, my heart, my reason for every step I took. She was my unbreakable vow, the promise I intended to keep, no matter what storm was hurtling toward us.

My assistant librarian approached, her brow furrowed with the responsibility we shared. "Sam, are you okay? You seem—"

"Focused," I interjected before she could finish. It wasn't a lie, but it wasn't the complete truth either. "We've got work to do, right?" I had to push all these feelings down.

"Right," she agreed, though her eyes lingered on me a moment longer, as if trying to decipher the story behind my carefully constructed walls.

"Okay, let's get everything back in order. Maybe track down some air freshener?" I said with a laugh that sounded fake, even to me.

"Definitely," she replied before moving off to

attend to the misplaced chairs and scattered belong-ings left in the wake of the evacuation.

Evan's sudden reappearance was a plot twist in the steady narrative I had written for myself and my daughter—a narrative where stability and safety were paramount, where the wild cards of wealthy families and old flames had no place.

CHAPTER 2

Evan

The moment my boots hit the pavement, I was zeroed in. The call came from the local library, and the monitoring system indicated the presence of smoke.

I'd only been in Minden for a few weeks as the Assistant Chief, and I was still operating as a member of the responding crew so I could learn the dynamics of the department. The combination of paid and volunteer staffing was new to me and posed an interesting challenge. Chicago was familiar, but it had become increasingly difficult to find anyone who could see beyond my last name.

Captain Parker was off duty, so I took point, quickly directing my team of two. My eyes traced the small crowd, assessing the scene. "Who's in charge here?"

"That would be me," a small voice said.

SHE STEPPED FORWARD. And for the first time ever as a firefighter, I lost focus on the call I was responding to. All I could see was her. It'd been almost fifteen years. My heart thundered against my ribs, as though it was desperate to break free, and I was frozen, caught in a torrent of emotions. Longing tangled up with confusion, a mess of threads I thought I'd tucked away. I had to be hallucinating, because there was no way this was–

"SAM?"

HER NAME SLIPPED from my lips, and my fingers reached toward her, unbidden.

HER STEP backward was the dousing of icy sanity I needed, and somehow I managed to hear what she said about the fire. Nothing major. Everyone was out.

MY MIND WAS REELING, but she wouldn't give me anything. Her face was frustratingly devoid of emotion, whereas I was vacillating rapidly between disbelief, joy, and anger with every beat of my traitorous heart.

"Mercer, you good?" one of the guys called out, jolting me back.

I nodded, but my gaze lingered on Sam, tracing the familiar lines of her face, the set of her shoulders. My mind hurtled back through time, racing down the years to when it was just the two of us. One blessed week together before sorrow and regret carved deep grooves into my life.

"Sam," I whispered under my breath, her name feeling both foreign and achingly familiar on my tongue.

The weight of guilt was a heavy cloak around my shoulders as I took those first tentative steps toward her. It had been years, but the past had a way of holding on, its grip steadfast. I'd never been able to shake it.

"We really appreciate the quick response from

Minden's finest. I'll be over here with my staff waiting for the all clear."

JUST LIKE THAT, she dismissed me with a few words–pleasantries she would offer any other fire-fighter. They cut like a scalpel. I didn't want cold and impersonal with her. I never had.

I paused, swallowing hard. My hands, calloused from a career of wrapping hoses and climbing ladders, fumbled at my sides, useless in this personal crisis. Even my faith, which had always been my compass through the smoky uncertainties of life, felt a tad shaky right now.

"I'll come find you." My words sank heavy into my gut, so similar to the words I'd said to her the night of the fire. But no matter how hard I had looked since then, I'd never been able to track down Samantha Brown.

And now here she was.

Reluctantly, I turned back to my team, and we ran a cursory check of the library, using the heat sensing camera to make sure there were no surprises hiding behind the walls. It was just the microwave, like Samantha had said.

When the all clear was given, my fellow firefighters packed up the truck. My gaze lingered on Samantha, the woman who had filled my world with color and light before everything dimmed. There's so much I wanted to say, to explain, maybe even to ask for forgiveness, but those words felt like a bridge too far, one that perhaps shouldn't be crossed again.

It was probably for the best. Whatever remnants of affection she might harbor for me were better left untouched. I was not the man she deserved—never had been. My actions the night of the fire proved that.

The Mercer name might have carried weight in Chicago, but here, in this painfully honest moment, I felt the full burden of the Mercer legacy. Wealth and influence are poor substitutes for true worthiness.

And the way she'd obviously been less than thrilled to see me again was just another confirmation.

"Be happy, Samantha," I said finally, a mere exhale carried away by the breeze. And with that, I turned back to my duties, to the life I'd chosen—a life of service, a penance that never quite absolved the guilt or filled the hollow spaces where love used to live.

Later in my shift, I could still feel the ember of her presence, smoldering somewhere deep within, flickering with every beat of my heart. She was here in Minden, after all these years of looking for her. I was back at the station, navigating through the routine of cleaning equipment and checking gear, but part of me was still out there on that quiet street with her only a few feet away.

Hours passed, or maybe minutes—it was hard to tell when your mind was elsewhere—and then she was there again, materializing in the doorway of the fire station like I'd summoned her from my fantasies. She had changed. The prim librarian outfit from earlier had been replaced with jeans and dressy blouse. I couldn't say which one drove me crazier.

Samantha stood rigid, holding a basket that seemed to weigh more than its contents would suggest. I flashed a wry smile, one I was sure appeared far more confident than I felt. "Well, what do we have here?"

She sighed, her annoyance and discomfort obvious. "Welcome to Minden. As a member of the town welcome committee, I am supposed to deliver this to you." Her voice was a tightrope, balancing between cold courtesy and the warmth I remembered. She's reciting a well-rehearsed line, as though it was taking every bit of control she has.

She extended the basket toward me and I grabbed it, ignoring the way my fingers trailed over hers. The woven fibers of the welcome basket scratched against my hands, making me miss the softness in her touch.

"The town welcome committee?" I asked, desperate to draw out this interaction as long as I could.

SHE NODDED. "Someone said you'd gotten an apartment in town, but we weren't sure of your address. So the committee suggested I bring it here to the station."

"Well, thank you."

"Of course," she said, her smile as taut as a freshly wound clock.

The air between us was thick with things unsaid, with the history that coiled around us like smoke from a fire long extinguished. She was here out of obligation, perhaps, or maybe curiosity. Either way, a bitterness lurked beneath her politeness. I grappled with the silence stretching out, trying to stitch it closed with words from a time when silence between us was a stranger.

"Sam, I just—"

"Save it, Evan." Her words sliced through the air, each syllable iced with a bitterness that sent a shiver down my spine. I stood there, in the middle of Minden's fire station, holding the welcome wagon gift like an accusation.

"Oooh, are those bagels from Danielle's place?" Elijah Woods walked by, grabbing the basket from my arms without waiting for permission. "Score!"

I barely gave him a glance as he started pulling food out of the basket and ripping into it. Instead, I searched her face for a sign of the warmth I once knew, but I only saw the same passive professionalism she'd shown at the library earlier. "I thought maybe we could talk about—"

"There's nothing to discuss." Samantha folded her arms, her posture rigid like the spines of the well-ordered books she guarded so carefully.

My mouth was dry, and I swallowed hard against the knot forming in my throat. I wanted to breach the chasm between us with words, but they faltered and crumbled before they could reach her. "I know I can't change the past, but—"

"Exactly," she interjected sharply, her eyes avoiding mine, as if the sight of me might unravel her composure. "You can't." The words were clipped, and she stepped back, retreating into the armor of her composure.

I nodded slowly, the weight of our history

pressing on my chest. The silence stretched between us, heavy with all the things left unsaid. I saw the finality in her stance, the resolve in her eyes.

She hated me.

The word 'sorry' sat on the tip of my tongue, but even that felt woefully inadequate. It's a bandage offered to a wound I never saw heal, one I inflicted with choices reluctantly made.

The crackle of the dispatcher's voice over the radio sliced through my contemplation. "Station Two, respond."

Duty called, but my feet dragged across the polished floor of the firehouse, each step heavy with a reluctance that anchored me to this spot. I glanced back at Samantha, her silhouette framed by the doorway, as rigid and impenetrable as the walls around us.

"Station Two," I replied mechanically into my radio, my gaze lingering on her for a moment longer than necessary. With a deep breath, I tore my eyes away and stepped into the boots of responsibility. The familiar weight of my gear settled onto my shoulders, a comforting burden compared to the weight of our unfinished business.

Sam could shut me out as much as she wanted. I hadn't been here long, but I already knew that

Minden was an exceptionally small town. She couldn't avoid me forever.

I WOULDN'T FORCE her into anything, but she deserved to know that she meant something to me back then. I wasn't the kind of guy for a one-night stand. I'd planned to wait until marriage, but I'd let myself take things too far. Still, if the fire hadn't—

I PUSHED down that line of thought. Thinking about what-ifs and could-have-beens was a waste of time.

THE CLUB BATHROOM HAPPENED. The fire happened. My brother happened.

AND THEN, she had vanished before I could apologize for taking advantage of her.

I WASN'T GOING to let her disappear again. Good thing Minden didn't have very many places to hide.

CHAPTER 3

Evan

The carefree girl who'd danced on Florida's white sands seemed worlds away from the librarian meticulously typing in front of me. Her appearance was carefully curated. Not that the prim and proper button-up blouse did anything to hide her curves or detract from her natural beauty. She even had a few strands of gray hair sparkling against the rest of her dark locks, pulled back tightly to the nape of her neck.

How was it that Samantha Brown, with her tidy bun and glasses perched on her nose, was the same girl who'd worn the black bikini and cutoff shorts I'd tackled into the waves?

"Libraries sure have changed since I last stepped

into one," I ventured, trying to bridge an ocean of history with levity and awkward small talk.

"And yet, quiet is still a requirement," she replied without looking up, the briefest quirk of her lips betraying her amusement at her own quip. She had this authoritative librarian thing down pat. And I was totally loving it.

"So, do I need a library card, or can I check you out another way?"

Had I really just said that? I cringed, looking away as my cheeks flushed. My brother would be laughing his butt off if he heard me.

The thought sobered my flirty thoughts. Before we went to the club that night, I'd gone golfing with him. He had even told me that he liked Sam. He said she brought out the real Evan.

Her eyes flickered to mine, a wrinkle deepening between them. "The borrowing limits on our library cards include twenty books and ten movies, audio-books, or CDs."

I let out a low whistle. Okay then. No more librarian pickup lines.

"Okay, I'd like a library card."

Without even looking, she slid a form across the desk, and I moved to the side to fill it out as she helped the next patron. She was all smiles and sugar with the preschool-aged boy, and I couldn't help but be jealous. A fact that boded well for my sanity, for sure.

"Any plans for updating the kids section?" the mother asked, her voice hopeful as she gestured toward the back corner, where I could see a faded mural and worn chairs. "The one in Greencastle just got an awesome storytime stage."

Samantha's lips thinned, her professional mask slipping just enough to reveal a glimpse of frustration. "I've been pushing for a renovation for years. New books, updated furniture..." She sighed, catching herself. "But funding is always the hurdle."

"Such a shame," the mom murmured, her toddler tugging impatiently on her sleeve.

An older gentleman walked up, obviously overhearing the last bit. "Yes, it would be nice," he said in a tone that sounded like he was discussing the weather rather than the future of the children's area. "But with the budget we have, dreams are all they'll ever be." He proceeded to step behind the desk and sit at the computer next to Sam. I eyed his nametag while pretending to focus on my form.

Patrick Henley, Library Director. Her boss, perhaps?

His dismissive comment hung in the air, and

Samantha's shoulders tensed while she finished scanning the stack of picture books. I felt a tightness in my chest, the same protective instinct that had me charging into burning buildings.

Why did this matter to me? I had no real stake in the children's section at this tiny library, and yet the hint of Samantha's disappointment bothered me. I shrugged off the feeling; I was here for a library card, not to get involved in municipal funding issues.

"Thanks, Sam. Tell Sophia I said hello," the young mother said before she led the little boy by the hand toward the door.

Samantha stiffened. "I will," she replied, but the warmth that usually accompanied such exchanges was noticeably absent. Her eyes didn't meet mine.

Sophia... The name echoed in my head, stirring up a whirlwind of questions. Who was Sophia? A friend? I could have asked, pushed her for an answer. But something in Samantha's guarded posture told me not to—told me she wasn't ready for me to know anything personal about her. My eyes flew to her left hand, reassuring me I hadn't missed a wedding ring there.

Still pretending to fill out the short form, I observed the strained interaction between her and the director. He was leaning over her desk now, flipping through some papers with an air of authority that seemed unnecessary given the quiet efficiency with which she worked.

"Make sure these are filed correctly, Samantha. And avoid engaging in idle chit-chat about financing; it's not professional," he chided without even a glance in her direction.

"Of course, Mr. Henley," she replied, every word measured and controlled. But her hands betrayed her, clenching ever so slightly before returning to the keyboard.

Watching them, I recognized the subtle dance of power and resistance, a dynamic far too familiar from the high-stakes world of my family's expectations.

I slid my completed form across the desk. "All set."

"Just need your proof of address," she prompted, her fingers poised over the keyboard after typing in the information I'd provided.

"Right. 42 Westbrook Lane, Unit C." I handed her my utility bill, glad I'd thought to grab it.

Something flashed across her face that I couldn't identify. But as quickly as it had come, it was shuttered behind her implacable mask. She typed in the address and hit a few more buttons, then grabbed a piece of paper from the printer beside her desk.

"All set. Here's your temporary card." She slid the paper across the desk, our fingertips nearly brushing, though she quickly pulled hers out of reach.

"Guess I'm officially a patron now. Do I get another welcome basket? Maybe a complimentary bookmark?"

"Budget cuts," she said, but this time the smile reached her eyes. "You'll have to make do with free knowledge and the occasional late fee."

"Personal tour?" My hopeful tone betrayed my desperation. Why wouldn't she give me even a passing glance?

She pointed to various areas around the room, never leaving her seat. "Fiction, non-fiction, computers, kids, young adults. Upstairs are meeting rooms and reference materials like periodicals, local records, and genealogy resources." Her smirk told me she knew the game I was playing and that she was determined to win it.

"Fair enough," I conceded, holding onto the fleeting warmth of her gaze like a lifeline.

"Listen, Samantha," I started, my voice barely above a whisper, "I wanted to say—"

"It's in the past, Mr. Mercer," she said, each word clipped and precise as she rearranged a stack of books on her left. "Let's keep our interactions professional, please." There was a sorrow in her eyes, the same sadness and regret I saw in my own expression every day.

I swallowed hard, the taste of regret bitter on my tongue. It was like trying to stitch a wound with barbed wire—the more I reached out, the deeper I cut myself. She was right, of course. Almost fifteen years had passed. What right did I have to dredge up old heartaches?

But there it was again—that familiar weight, compressing my chest until my breaths felt like sips through a cocktail straw. It seemed no amount of smoke I'd faced in burning buildings could suffocate the guilt that smoldered within me.

Was I trying to apologize to her? Or to assuage my own guilt? I wanted her to know that I wasn't a bad guy.

Of course, I had been having sex with her in a nightclub bathroom while my brother died in a fire across the building. So maybe that wasn't an achievable goal.

"Of course," I managed to choke out, the words heavy and hollow.

The fireman in me wanted to rescue her from any hint of sorrow, but the man in me knew better. How much of it had I been the cause of? Had she looked for me after the fire? Waited for my call? Even if my phone with her number hadn't been lost at the bottom of the Gulf of Mexico, would I have? Everything changed when I found out Mason had died. I should have been with him, but I'd been too busy selfishly betraying my own values and taking advantage of the innocent woman who was now sitting across from me.

Her fingers paused, and for a moment, I hoped for a look, a sign—anything to suggest she saw me as more than just another patron with overdue books.

"Your card will be mailed to you within five business days," she said, handing me a receipt with a practiced smile that didn't reach her eyes. "Is there anything else I can help you with?"

"Nope," I replied, popping the P, though my mind screamed a litany of unfinished sentences and unasked questions. I didn't need anything from her. Nothing except to understand why God had brought her back into my world. Was it simply that I needed to right the wrongs I had done back then? I'd confessed and repented that sin long ago. But I'd never made things right with Sam.

And so far, she didn't seem inclined to let me.

As I stepped away from the counter, the distance between us stretched beyond the physical space. It was filled with what-ifs and if-onlys, bridged only by the faintest glimmer of hope that maybe God had a plan for broken things.

And in that moment, I realized I cared about the answer more than I dared to admit.

I tucked the paper card in my wallet and rapped my knuckle on the desk before stepping away.

I lingered between the stacks of novels, pretending to browse the latest Charles Martin books. I told myself I should let Samantha be. The tight set of her shoulders, the measured cadence of her voice—it all spoke to a door firmly closed, a chapter she had no intention of reopening. And if she was determined to keep that door shut, who was I to pry it open?

It wasn't as though I were interested in rediscovering what we had. Truth be told, curiosity gnawed at my insides. It demanded answers to the mystery of Samantha's reaction, to the significance of Sophia, or anyone else that held a permanent spot in her life. I wanted to know everything about Samantha.

My curiosity was going to be the death of me. I cast one last glance over my shoulder as I edged toward the exit. I should leave her alone, but I wasn't sure I was strong enough to ignore the pull.

CHAPTER 4

Samantha

I absently stirred the pasta sauce on the stove, listening to Sophia hum to herself at the table while she tackled her homework. It was the very picture of a normal day. Except today proved, yet again, that things would no longer be normal around here.

Evan Mercer, of all people, had blown into Minden like a storm I'd never seen coming. It was bad enough that he was in town, but his library card application had revealed that he was also living practically right next door to me, in the same apartment complex. How was I supposed to keep Sophia a secret when he lived so close?

I could still feel the echo of his laughter as he stood before me earlier, winking while I processed his library card. His pickup lines, delivered with a flirtatious curve lifting the corner of his mouth. I couldn't help the amusement that bubbled up, but I squashed it. No, I wasn't going to let his charm ripple through the calm waters I'd worked so hard to still. Even if he was just as handsome and charming as ever.

Fourteen years ago, there had been something about Evan, the way he'd wrapped me in warmth and safety, how he made me laugh until my sides hurt. I remembered the sun-kissed days and whispered promises and how easily I fell for him.

I wasn't exactly the spring break vacation type, but my roommate had insisted. She paid for the entire hotel room and all the gas, which was the only way I would have been able to afford a trip like that. My scholarship had barely covered tuition and room and board. The dining hall food everyone complained about felt like heaven compared to the empty cabinets I'd left behind at home.

On the beach, it felt so good to let loose and pretend I was just another college girl, carefree and fun. To ignore the stress of maintaining my grades and ignoring angry text messages from my family harassing me for abandoning them.

Evan, with his broad shoulders and golden-boy

smile, had been another piece of that imaginary existence. Smart, funny, charming. I was caught by his spell so quickly. He promised me forever. Looking back, I could see my naivete. Five days? And I thought he wanted forever? I was foolish.

But I wouldn't trade the result for anything. Sophia was my life. And now, Evan's sudden presence threatened to unravel the secrets I'd held close for fourteen long years.

The Chicago trust fund frat boy might have stumbled back into my life, but there was no way I would let him disrupt the peace I'd found here—or the future I promised to protect for Sophia.

"Mom! The water!"

I jumped, grabbing the pot handle and turning down the burner, but not before a sizzling hiss of water met the stovetop. Steam curled into the air, and I winced.

"Ooops," I muttered, reaching for a towel to wipe up the mess.

Sophia sighed dramatically from where she stood at the kitchen counter. "You okay?" she asked, arching an eyebrow at me.

I forced a smile, ignoring the knot in my stomach. "Just a long day."

Sophia's sharp brown eyes studied me, too wise for her fourteen years. "You're lying to me."

My fingers tightened around the wooden spoon as I stirred the pasta. "I don't know what you mean. Fix the salad, would you?" Maybe giving her a job would distract her from this line of questioning.

Sophia snorted. "Fine, but I'm not dropping this." She pulled veggies from the fridge and grabbed the salad bowl and wooden tongs. "Is it money?"

I inhaled deeply, stirring the noodles as if they held all the answers. "No, it's not."

Sophia hummed in a way that told me she didn't buy it. "Uh-huh. You know, Lola said that you can sell plasma if we need to make money."

Despite myself, I let out a soft laugh. "Well, Lola is technically right, though I won't be doing that any time soon."

"So what is it?"

I exhaled, my heart aching at how much she was growing up—and at the truth I was still keeping from her. "I promise I'll tell you when it makes sense."

Sophia rolled her eyes. "Whatever. That means you won't."

I smiled, ignoring the bit of attitude. I knew she was only pushing because she cared about me. I hated lying to her, but I couldn't tell her the truth yet. I would, though. I just had to figure out how.

The sun was bright against the pale blue sky when I stepped out into the still, cool air of the parking lot the next morning. The familiar distant rattle of the train through town and the subtle rustle of leaves in the early-morning breeze promised a day like any other in Minden's quiet routine.

I dropped my bag in the passenger seat of my car and then turned the key. Instead of the engine's confident roar, all I got were sputters and half-hearted coughs from my old sedan. A sense of frustration knotted in my stomach; today was not the day for this. I was already running late. Sophia had overslept and I barely got her on the bus on time.

"Great," I muttered, stepping out of the car to confront the stubborn machine head-on. My hands felt clumsy and uncertain as they fumbled to find the hood latch. It finally gave way with a metallic yawn, revealing the chaotic innards of my vehicle. I hated to admit I had no idea what I was looking for.

I peered into the mechanical abyss, trying to summon knowledge from a car maintenance video I'd watched years ago. But everything blurred into a conglomeration of pipes, wires, and reservoirs, none of which sparked recognition or understanding.

I felt the pressure mounting, the weight of the day's schedule pressing down on me. Being late was not an option—Mr. Henley already hated me. I was pushing for a raise, and he'd love nothing more than to blame my tardiness for my lack of career progression.

We needed that five percent bump, though. With each passing minute, I could feel the opportunity slipping through my fingers.

I stood back from the car, debating my options with my hands on my hips, when the sound of footsteps approached.

"Trouble?" His voice was like the rumble of a distant storm—calm but hinting at powerful forces beneath. I didn't have to turn around to know it was Evan; his presence seemed to charge the air.

Because I couldn't resist the pull, I glanced over my shoulder, taking in the sight of him—still clad in his MRFD T-shirt, tucked neatly into his dark blue pants.

"Car won't start," I replied curtly, my pride flaring up like a match struck against a rough surface. "And I'm perfectly capable of handling it."

"Of course you are." Evan's words were gentle, no trace of condescension. He stopped beside me, gazing down at the open hood with an assessing eye. "I just got off a twenty-four-hour shift, so I can either continue on to my apartment, which is apparently quite close to yours…" There was a pause, a moment of unspoken negotiation. "Or, you can let me check on your car."

I hesitated, caught between the need for punctuality and the stubbornness that had become my shield. With a reluctant nod, I stepped aside, granting him access to the engine.

"On one condition: you listen while I talk," he said with a smirk.

I narrowed my eyes. "Talk about what?"

Evan didn't answer right away. Instead, he leaned over the engine, inspecting wires and connections as if he had all the time in the world. His T-shirt stretched across his back, highlighting the strength beneath, and for a split second, I hated that I noticed. Hated that even after all these years, my body still reacted to him before my brain could remind me why I shouldn't.

I checked my watch, tapping my foot against the pavement. "Evan—"

"Relax," he murmured, tightening something near the battery. "I know you're in a hurry. Just hear me out."

I crossed my arms, bracing myself. "Fine. Say whatever it is you think I need to hear."

He exhaled, like he'd expected me to fight him on this. "Back in Florida—"

My stomach twisted. "Please don't."

Evan paused, glancing at me. "Samantha." His voice softened in a way that made my throat tighten. "That week… it wasn't nothing to me. I looked for you, you know," Evan said quietly, his gaze not meeting mine. "After that week… after everything went down."

"You looked for me," I repeated, not comprehending.

"I needed to know you were okay, to apologize for leaving things… unresolved."

"Unresolved," I repeated, tasting the bitterness of the word. The past was a Pandora's box, and he was prying it open with every sincere syllable.

"I know you don't want to hear this," he continued, finally looking up at me. Those kind eyes searched mine, seeking forgiveness or understanding—I couldn't tell which. "But I needed to say it. To face the fact that I—"

"Left," I interrupted, my voice steadier than I felt. "You left without a word."

A pained expression flitted across his face,

acknowledging the accusation. "I did. And I've regretted it every day since."

My heart fought a battle against the walls I'd meticulously constructed. How easy it would be to let him see the waves his reappearance had caused, to let him in on the secret that had shaped my life for fourteen years. Yet I couldn't—wouldn't dismantle the fortress protecting my daughter's world.

"Regret doesn't change the past," I said, my tone clipped, more a defense mechanism than conviction. Each word was a brick laid atop the last, keeping the truth buried deep.

"Doesn't mean we can't learn from it, try to make things right," he countered, his resilience evident even as he reached for another wire, his focus shifting back to the task at hand.

"Sometimes things are better left alone," I whispered, not sure if I meant to convince him or myself. I watched as he worked, his movements deft and purposeful, yet beneath his calm exterior I sensed the same tumult that churned within me.

I gritted my teeth. "It was fourteen years ago." My heart pounded painfully. I wanted to ask how hard he'd really looked, to tell him he'd obviously given up too fast. "When?"

"What?"

"When did you look for me?"

His jaw clenched as he ducked into the driver's seat. "A few months later," he admitted. "But I was–"

"It's fine," I dismissed his excuses. A few months before he bothered trying to find me? By then, I was trying to hide my baby bump under hoodies during the summer semester.

The engine sputtered as he turned the key again, then it roared to life.

Evan stepped back out, wiping his hands on his pants. "Loose connection. Should be good for now, but you might want to get it checked out."

I swallowed past the lump in my throat. "Thanks."

He studied me, his gaze searching. "I'm not going anywhere this time, Samantha."

My fingers tightened on the door handle. "I don't need you to stay."

His jaw flexed, but he just stepped back. "Drive safe."

I nodded sharply, sliding into the car. I slammed the door shut, sealing myself off from his presence, his help, his past. I didn't dare glance in the rearview mirror as I drove away; the sight of him might unravel the thin threads holding me together.

The drive was a blur, my focus fragmented by the

whirlwind of emotions that swirled within. Anger, fear, longing—each vying for the lead in my chaotic thoughts. And beneath it all, the steady drumbeat of my primary purpose: to protect Sophia at all costs.

Parking outside the library, the building's familiar facade offered no solace today. I sat for a moment, hands resting lifelessly on the steering wheel. The weight of secrets pressed down on me like the heavy Midwestern humidity that would build throughout the day.

Fourteen years of carefully constructed walls, fourteen years of guarding the truth with a ferocity born of necessity. And now, Evan Mercer, with his kind eyes and calloused hands, threatened to bring it all crashing down.

CHAPTER 5
Samantha

I couldn't catch a break. It was like everywhere I went in this town, there he was. I barely registered the familiar scent of roasted beans and cinnamon that usually greeted me like an old friend. Because even *my* coffee shop had been invaded. My town, my library, my apartment complex. And now my coffee shop? I wanted to stomp my foot like my teenage daughter did when she thought I was being unfair. Because life was certainly being unfair right now.

There he was, sitting by the window, his tall frame slightly hunched over a steaming mug, his Bible open on the table in front of him. I rolled my eyes. The man was my baby daddy, for crying out loud. What an upstanding example of Christianity.

Ugh. That was catty, and obviously I knew that Christians made mistakes. I was the unmarried single mom, after all. But come on.

"Can I get you the usual, Samantha?" the barista's voice cut through my trance.

His eyes flew up at her words and I quickly turned away, embarrassed to be caught studying him.

"Um, yes, thanks," I murmured, quickly paying for my coffee and waiting at a nearby table.

I scrolled aimlessly on my phone, desperately trying to ignore his presence a few feet away.

"Mind if I join you?" I glanced up to find him standing next to me, his Bible now tucked under his arm and his coffee in his hand.

"Sure," I answered, my voice a controlled whisper, though inside, I was screaming.

"Thanks," Evan replied, pulling up a chair. His eyes lifted to meet mine with a warmth that I wished didn't stir something within me.

We sat there, surrounded by the low hum of other patrons' conversations and the clinking of ceramic on wood, enveloped in an awkward silence. Holly brought my coffee, and I clung to it like a life raft.

I could feel Evan's gaze on me, patient and

expectant.

Evan cleared his throat, a subtle signal that he was about to steer us away from the precipice of silence. Except, there was nothing for us to talk about. We weren't friends, and I couldn't pretend we were.

"I should go," I said, pushing to my feet.

"Oh..." He almost looked disappointed. "Can I walk you out?"

"No," I said quickly—too quickly perhaps, feeling the façade crack just a bit. My gaze dropped to the table, focusing on the wood grain patterns as I fought to keep my emotions from spilling over.

Evan reached out, as if to bridge the gap, but stopped short. "If there's something you need to talk about—" he began, but I cut him off.

"Really, I'm fine." The lie tasted bitter on my tongue, but I swallowed it down with another sip of coffee. My heart hammered away, protesting the falsehoods, but I couldn't afford the truth—not yet, not now. "I just need to go."

I could admit to myself that I was running. Except, there was really nowhere to run in Minden.

I managed to avoid Evan for the next few days. But a few nights later, after a long day of hauling boxes of old encyclopedias to the storage shed, I snuck out of the apartment after Sophia went to bed. The apartment complex had a postage-stamp-sized pool that Sophia loved, but it was the hot tub calling my name that night.

I dropped my towel on the chair and eased into the warmth of the hot tub, groaning at the almost painful heat. I found a seat and tipped my head back on the stone edge, letting the hot water loosen the tightness of my back and shoulders. The day's tension ebbed away with each ripple. Then a familiar voice sliced through the tranquility.

"Samantha?"

My eyes snapped open, and my heart kicked against my ribs. Evan stood at the edge of the hot tub, his arms crossed over his chest, his expression unreadable in the dim glow of the pool lights. Water droplets clung to his skin, and his damp hair told me he'd already been swimming.

"Didn't peg you for a rule breaker," he said, one brow lifting.

I frowned. "What are you talking about?"

His lips twitched like he was fighting a smirk. "Pool closes at ten."

I glanced toward the sign near the gate, scowling when I saw the posted hours. "Seriously?"

Evan shrugged, stepping closer. "Don't worry. I

won't tell—if you let me join you."

I shut my eyes, ignoring the temptation to trace his abs with my gaze. "It's a free country," I replied.

"If I get in, are you going to leave?"

My lips twitched. "Maybe."

He sighed. "Does it have to be like this?"

"Like what?"

"You avoiding me at every turn? I said I was sorry, Sam. I know it doesn't make up for the way I disappeared, but it's true. That night…" He bit off his words. "That night changed everything for me."

I barely contained the scoff that built in my lungs. It changed everything for him? I was the one who walked away as a single mom. What could have honestly changed for him?

My curiosity got the better of me and I whispered the question, my eyes opening at the sound of him slipping into the water. "How?"

He took a moment to answer, his head tipping back to look at the sky, exposing his throat and causing the muscles at the base of his neck to flex.

"The fire." His voice was quiet, almost drowned out by the bubbling water.

I stilled. A strange prickle ran down my spine. "The one at the club?"

He nodded, dragging a hand through his wet

hair. His jaw clenched so tight I swore I could hear his teeth grind. "Yeah." He let out a sharp breath and finally looked at me, his gaze filled with something raw and unguarded. "That night didn't just change everything, Sam. It wrecked me."

I swallowed hard. "I don't—"

"My brother was there," he said, cutting me off. "Mason."

I blinked. "Your brother?" I met his brother briefly that week. I remembered his blonde hair and the way he'd teased Evan about me before we'd ditched him on the boardwalk.

He gave a hollow laugh and tipped his head back against the stone edge. "Yeah. He was barely eighteen. Just a stupid kid looking to have fun." His voice wavered, but he pushed forward. "I brought him on the trip, did you know that? Told him we'd have a great time. Promised my parents I'd look out for him."

A knot formed in my stomach. I already knew where this was going.

"I still feel like the night is all hazy. I know we were in the bathroom when the fire broke out," he continued, his voice lower now, like he hated saying the words. "You and me." He gave me a brief, unreadable look before staring at the water again. "I remember the smoke, the alarm blaring. The whole place was crazy. People screaming, shoving—" He exhaled sharply. "I lost you in the crowd by the exit. But I had to find him."

My fingers tightened on the hot tub's edge.

"I searched for him," he whispered. "Fought my way through the smoke, tried to get back inside, but security dragged me out. And when the fire was finally out…" His voice broke. "He didn't make it."

The silence that followed was suffocating.

I felt cold despite the steaming water. My memories were hazy too. Many times over the years, I'd wondered if someone hadn't spiked my drink. Not Evan. No, that thought had never crossed my mind. I might have only known him a week, but I *had* known him. Some of his more obnoxious friends had mentioned that we needed to loosen up. A comment that could have been innocent. Or not.

After the fire, I watched the news, cried about the people who didn't make it out. He'd been with me by the exit, so even though I'd never heard from him over the years, I'd never really considered that he hadn't made it out. But I never imagined he'd lost someone. I'd been so heartbroken when I never heard from him. And then, after I found out about Sophia, I became terrified that I would.

"I didn't know," I whispered.

He gave a tight, humorless smile. "Of course, you didn't. I didn't have a way to tell you." His hands clenched beneath the surface. "By the time I could think straight, you were gone. I tried, Sam. I tried to find you."

I looked down, guilt twisting inside me. I had spent years believing I was the only one left to pick up the broken pieces of that night. But Evan... he had been carrying his own wreckage all along.

"You tried to find me?"

He grimaced, running a hand over his face. "Yes, of course I did. Sam, I just wanted to talk to you. I felt like the biggest jerk in the world," he said with a groan. "What happened in that bathroom... I wasn't... I'm not the kind of guy who does that. I didn't–don't–do hookups." He jerked a shoulder. "Maybe it doesn't matter now. After all, it's been fourteen years, but I wanted you to know. I wanted to apologize. It never should have happened."

A thousand thoughts flickered through my mind. He regretted it. He claimed he didn't do hookups, but somehow we ended up in the club bathroom of all places? I'd spent fourteen years ashamed of the way my daughter came into the world. But I could never regret it.

Evan wasn't done. "I hired an investigator about a year after the fire. To track you down."

My blood turned to ice, despite the heat of the water. "You did?" The words squeezed through the tightness in my throat. It wasn't as though I'd hidden from him. I wouldn't even know how.

He huffed and lifted one corner of his lips. "Yeah. Apparently, Samantha Brown is common enough he was never able to track you down. Not that I had much to give him to go on. I knew you were from Indiana and went to school at DePaul. But he could never track you down."

I pressed my eyes shut, my breath escaping in a rush. I didn't know whether to cry or praise God for the misunderstanding. "I went to DePauw University, Evan."

"Right. DePaul."

"DePauw," I corrected. "With a W."

I glanced back at him then. His brow was furrowed in confusion. "What?"

"DePauw University. It's in Greencastle." Twenty minutes up the road. Other than my big trip to Florida as a college student, my world remained very small.

Evan sat up so fast, the water splashed up my neck. "You weren't in Chicago?"

I shook my head slowly. "I've never even been to Chicago," I admitted. I hadn't had the opportunity before that trip to Florida, and I had certainly avoided the city ever since, knowing what I did about the Mercer family.

Evan gritted his teeth. I watched in shock as he dropped his head into the water, covering his face. I could hear a muffled sound, and a deluge of bubbles engulfed the sides of his face, like he was yelling under the water. Then, he lifted his head and ran his hands down his face, wiping away the droplets.

"Ummm, what was that?"

Evan sighed and muttered. "DePauw University. All this time I could have found you and it turns out I'm just an idiot."

My lips twitched, tugging into a reluctant smile. "It's an understandable mistake."

He shook his head. "I remember every single thing you said to me that week. But I missed that."

"It's not a big deal," I said. "Like you said... it's been a long time."

He didn't answer, and the silence settled comfortably around us. It felt like something was resolved now. He'd said what he needed to. He'd apologized. But my own secrets were still there, palpable as ever.

"Getting late," I murmured eventually, more to remind myself than him. I rose from the comforting heat of the hot tub, bracing against the cool night air as I wrapped myself in my towel.

In the glow of the patio lights, Evan's profile was etched with lines of thoughtfulness, his kind eyes shadowed by the weight of things left unsaid. "Let me walk you back," he offered, and something in the simple kindness of his gesture unraveled a thread of my resolve. He rubbed his hair with the towel, then slung it around his hips, his washboard abs deeply defined in the reflection and shadows of the dim lights.

"I'm fine," I insisted. The last thing I needed was him to see something at my apartment that would tip him off about Sophia. Was her bike still in the front? Would she have woken while I was gone? I left her a note, but what if she opened the door?

"It's dark. Better safe than sorry," he said with a crooked grin.

"It's also Minden," I replied with a laugh, trying to cover my hesitation. "I know you're new here, but surely you're aware of our low crime rate."

"Low isn't zero," he said firmly.

I sighed as though I was annoyed, but I couldn't

deny the little gleeful thrill his protectiveness sent through my body.

We reached the pool gate, his arm brushing against mine as he held the gate open —a touch that sent whispers of electricity skittering across my skin.

"Thanks," I said, suddenly conscious of the proximity.

His smile was gentle, but it tugged at something inside me, leaving me yearning for a reality where complications didn't loom over every interaction.

The air seemed to grow denser with each step we took toward my apartment, a pressure building in my chest that mirrored the tightening grip of anxiety. I couldn't shake the image of Sophia peeking through the window, Evan seeing her curious eyes on us and dunking me headfirst into a lifetime's worth of questions I wasn't prepared to answer.

As we approached my apartment door, I hesitated. "Here we are," I announced prematurely, halting a good few paces away from the actual door. The words tumbled out, clipped and rushed. "Thanks for the escort."

He paused, a small furrow forming between his brows as he searched my face. "Sure thing. Is everything okay?"

"Everything's fine," I assured him too quickly, the lie leaving a bitter taste in my mouth. I fumbled with the keys, not trusting myself to meet his gaze any longer. "Good night, Evan."

"Good night, Samantha," he replied. "I'm glad we got to finally get everything out in the open tonight. I hope you'll forgive me for the way things happened, if you haven't already."

With every word, he twisted the knife just a little deeper. I forced a smile, then hurried inside before I could betray how much he'd gotten to me.

The moment the door closed behind me, I leaned against it, the cool surface doing nothing to quell the fluttering in my stomach. The silence of the apartment pressed down on me.

I slid down to the floor, wrapping my arms around my knees, trying to ground myself. But my thoughts wouldn't stop spinning. How quickly he slipped past my defenses, just like before. And how, no matter what we'd said tonight, the biggest truth of all still hung between us.

The knowledge of Sophia's existence—and Evan's ignorance of his connection to her. The guilt twisted inside me.

"I hope you can forgive *me*," I whispered into the stillness, though whether the plea was to Evan, to

Sophia, or to God, I couldn't say. Maybe all three. Only silence answered back—a blank canvas upon which my doubts and desires waged their silent war.

My faith, usually my compass, now felt like another burden. The principles I held dear demanded an honesty that would shatter the fragile peace I'd built around my daughter.

I'd told myself that keeping the secret was to protect Sophia, to shield her from the complexities of a past she didn't need to navigate. To keep Evan's powerful family from taking her away from me. But maybe it was also to protect myself from the vulnerability of opening my heart again—the possibility that I would be broken beyond repair this time.

The stakes were too high, the risks too great. I rose slowly. Tomorrow would come. And sooner or later, the truth would too. I could forgive him. But even if he found out about Sophia, I didn't have to let Evan back into my heart. I wasn't the same scared twenty-one-year-old who'd been afraid of the Mercer name. I had built a good life for Sophia. I had a degree and a good job.

And even though the bills had a tendency to pile up, especially the hospital bills, I wouldn't let him or his family push me around. Sophia was mine.

CHAPTER 6

Evan

The drums from the high school marching band thrummed a patriotic heartbeat as I walked next to the fire engine in Minden's Fourth of July parade. It was only 10:30 in the morning, but the heat was already oppressive. I smiled at waving kids and passed out candy, but I found myself searching for Samantha in the crowd lining Main Street.

I shouldn't be looking for her. She'd made it quite clear that what had happened in our past was just that—in the past. Which was perfect, because I wasn't in the market for anything more. After the night in the hot tub, we crossed paths several times. A smile exchanged over late fees at the library, idle chatter about weather when we ran into each other at B&J Bistro, a polite wave in the parking lot of the apartment complex.

Every interaction somehow left me wanting to know more about the woman she was now. Wishing she would flash me a genuine smile instead of the polite-but-detached acknowledgement she'd offered. She'd given me nothing to indicate she wanted to see more of me, and yet as I scanned the crowd, she was the only one on my mind.

And then, there she was. Samantha stood in the back of the crowd in front of Bulldogs Bar and Grill. Her eyes flickered across the parade and spectators with amusement. Her hands clutched a small, well-loved novel, fingers marking a page as if she could slip back into its world at any moment.

Her gaze found mine across the distance, and for a fleeting second, something flickered in her eyes— recognition, or maybe surprise. But it was gone as quickly as it appeared, snuffed out like a candle in the wind. Her nod was cool, nonchalant, as though I was just another face in the uniformed sea of fire-fighters marching by.

I flashed her that smile—the one that used to come so easily but now felt like a relic of a happier Evan. I raised my hand high, a wave meant just for her. She didn't wave back.

I lowered my arm, a familiar weight settling on my chest. It was that same tightness that crept in during quiet nights alone, when the shadows of past mistakes stretched long across the walls of my empty apartment. Resolute, I squared my shoulders; I wouldn't let this setback quench the flame of determination kindling within me.

My steps carried me in her direction, and I passed out too much candy to the eager children swarming my legs, until my bucket was empty. "Sorry, kiddos. Here comes Jake." I gestured to Jake Barrett, a half block behind me. "He'll take care of you."

I glanced toward the truck, then stepped over the curb, squeezing through sets of camp chairs folks had set up. My heart thrummed louder than the drums as I came up next to Sam.

"Happy Fourth of July," I said, wishing I had a smoother greeting.

"Hey, Evan," she said, tucking a strand of hair behind her ear. Her eyes darted around the crowd. She seemed nervous. Was it just my presence?

"Having fun?"

She shrugged. "Sure. It's fun to see all the floats the businesses come up with."

I was going to comment on the float from Brand

New Landscaping that featured the whole crew of college guys dressed in hula skirts. They were obviously going for the "funniest float" award. I'd met Luke Brand when I first moved into town. He and his wife Charlotte led a Bible study for married couples.

But before I could say anything, a young girl darted up to us, drawing my attention from Sam to the miniature version standing a foot away.

"Can I go swimming at Ella's house?"

I was pretty sure my eyebrows had just relocated to somewhere behind my hairline. My gaze flew back to Sam's and found her entire focus on the teenage girl next to us.

"I'm not sure. Who else is going?"

"It's just Ella and Sarah and me. Please??" The girl was persistent.

Samantha sighed. "Okay, sure. Just have Ella's mom call me when I should pick you up. No later than five." Her voice rose at the end, since the girl had already run off. She lifted a hand in acknowledgement of Samantha's instructions.

I watched her retreat into the crowd, a flicker of familiarity igniting in my chest. Her expressive eyes, that easy smile—hadn't I seen them somewhere before? The feeling was disorienting, like a memory playing hide and seek just beyond the edge of recollection.

There was an unsettling familiarity in the way she had tossed her hair over her shoulder—a mirror image of a gesture I'd seen countless times before. My mouth went dry as the wheels turned in my head, churning through the murky waters of possibility.

Could she be her sister? No, Samantha never mentioned a sister. A cousin, perhaps? But no, that familial resemblance was too pronounced, too specific. It was like staring into the past, into a time capsule of memories I had tried so hard to bury beneath layers of ash and resolve.

Samantha turned back to me. "I should go," she said. Her voice was clipped and breathy, slightly panicky. "Enjoy the rest of your day." Without meeting my eyes, she turned and practically jogged down the block.

My tongue felt like lead in my mouth as I watched her leave. I couldn't form a single word, let alone voice the questions that were bubbling up inside, hot and acidic like the volcano I'd seen once in Hawaii.

The blast of a trumpet behind me jolted me back into the moment. I looked around to find that the firetruck was already a block ahead, about to turn the corner. With one final glance at Samantha's retreating figure, I turned the other way and jogged to meet up with my crew.

I felt strangely disassociated from the rest of the parade. Going through the motions, I continued to represent the Minden Rogers Fire Department. But my mind was a million miles away, stuck on the smiling, sassy face of a teenage girl.

Samantha had a daughter. She was young, but the resemblance to the younger version of Sam I remembered from Florida was undeniable. I was no expert at guessing the ages of young girls, but she looked to be no older than thirteen or fourteen. Maybe as young as eleven. Which either meant... No. There was no way Samantha could...

The parade had come to its exuberant finale, the final notes of the marching band dissolving into the applause and cheers of the town. Feeling a mixture of relief and restlessness, I peeled off from the procession with my fellow firefighters, our boots thudding in unison on the sun-warmed asphalt.

"Good turnout this year," remarked Chief Bergman, as he tugged off his helmet and wiped his brow with a handkerchief that had seen better days.

"Definitely," I agreed, trying to anchor myself in

the present moment, but my thoughts kept drifting like rogue embers back to Samantha and the girl —Sophia.

"Hey, Evan, you seemed a bit distracted out there," Jake said with a teasing voice. "Someone catch your eye?"

"Sort of," I admitted, my voice steady, despite the way my gut was swirling. My gaze flicked across the dispersing crowd, still half-expecting to see Samantha reappear. "Actually, you guys know Samantha Brown?"

"Librarian Samantha?" Nathan asked, squinting under the brim of his cap. "Sure, she's been here since forever. My kids love story time."

If I remembered correctly, Nathan had three boys. Kudos to him—and his wife. My brother and I were already a handful for our parents. I couldn't imagine adding another to the mix.

"Yeah, that's her," I said, feeling an odd mix of hesitation and desperation. How much information could I get without tipping my hand. "She has a daughter—Sophia, right?"

"Yep, she's like... thirteen? Kid's got her mom's brains, I'll tell ya," Eli replied, chuckling. "Got herself into the accelerated program at school. Carla is her teacher and can't say enough good things."

Carla was Eli's fiancée and a teacher at the middle school.

"Thirteen, huh?" My heart skipped a beat, the rhythm falling out of sync as if it sensed the impending revelation. "And no husband in the picture?"

"Never has been," Jake chimed in, his tone casual, unaware of the seismic shift occurring beneath my ribcage. "Just Samantha and her girl, as long as I've known 'em. Why? You looking to apply for the job?" He waggled his eyebrows at me.

"Bug off," I muttered, my mind churning like a storm surge threatening to breach its barriers. Thirteen. The number reverberated through me, each echo a hammer strike on the walls of my composure.

"Everything alright, Evan?" Chief's question was tinged with genuine concern, but I could only manage a tight-lipped smile.

"Fine," I answered, though nothing felt fine. Everything was tilting, the horizon of my understanding warping as pieces began to fit together with a precision that terrified me.

As they continued to banter about the day's success, I stood there, rooted in place, the chill of realization creeping up my spine. If Sophia was thirteen, then the timeline...

My breath hitched. Could it be? The mere possibility sent shivers down my arms, raising the hair on the back of my neck despite the July heat.

"Hey, you're coming for the barbecue at the station, right?" Nathan's voice cut through the fog of my thoughts.

"Uh, yeah," I managed to say, the word feeling like ash on my tongue. "Wouldn't miss it."

I scrubbed a hand over my face, the sweat mixing with the dust of the parade route on my skin. The laughter and chatter of my fellow firefighters filled the air as we walked toward the fire station for the barbecue. I should have been in the moment, celebrating the holiday with my crew, but my mind refused to let go of the tangle of possibilities that wrapped around my thoughts like thorny vines.

"Everything alright?" asked Eli, his brow creasing with concern. He was a jokester, but in the short time I had been in Minden, it seemed to me that Eli was the most perceptive firefighter in the station. He could always tell when something was off.

"Fine," I said, my voice steady despite the storm raging inside me. "Just tired. You know how it is."

But it wasn't fatigue that gnawed at me—it was the haunting suspicion that the girl with Samantha's eyes might be...could she really be mine? I pushed the thought down, trying to cage it like some wild animal that threatened to burst free at any moment.

The familiar smell of smoldering coals from the barbecue filled my nostrils as we arrived at the station, doing little to ease the tightness in my chest. I grabbed a plate, piling it high with food I didn't have an appetite for, while plastering on a smile that felt more like a grimace.

"Hey, Mercer, you're looking a bit pale, man," Eli joked, elbowing me gently. "You'd think you just ran into a burning building instead of walking a parade route."

"Guess I'm just not as young as I used to be," I quipped back, deflecting with humor—a skill honed through years of navigating both emotional and physical infernos.

As the sun blazed higher, the conversation turned to families and kids, a topic that would normally entertain me, despite the lack of children in my family. But not today. Today, each word about parenting was a stinging reminder of my own potential link to a child I knew nothing about.

I had to talk to her. I deserved to know the truth.

But what if the truth was that Samantha had hidden a daughter from me for over a decade? The thought made me nauseous, the burger turning to ash in my mouth.

"Mercer, you in for horseshoes?" someone called out, pulling me from my reverie.

"Count me in," I replied, setting my barely touched plate aside. I couldn't solve this tonight.

"You sure you know how to play?" Jake smirked. "Or do they just toss gold-plated horseshoes at country clubs in Chicago?"

"Yeah," Kyle added. "Pretty sure the only thing Mercer ever tossed growing up was caviar onto a cracker."

I snorted. "You guys are hilarious. Really. That's just ridiculous. Obviously, we had a guy to toss the caviar for us."

A round of groans and exaggerated eye rolls followed. I was well-practiced in deflecting jokes about my privileged upbringing. It was a hundred times worse in Chicago where I'd worked before. I could handle Minden's friendly ribbing.

"Figures," Kyle said. "Bet he had a personal horseshoe coach, too."

"Of course," I deadpanned. "Come on now. You tell yourself whatever it takes to stomach the devastating loss you're about to experience." With that parting shot, I let the horseshoe fly.

With a satisfying clank, it hit the post. For the next several hours, I lost myself in the camaraderie of my new station.

But if Samantha had been hiding Sophia from me? I made a silent vow to seek out the truth, no matter how much it burned.

CHAPTER 7

Samantha

I bolted from the parade like a startled deer, my heart thundering against my ribs so fiercely I could almost hear it over the marching band. The festive music in the distance faded as my thoughts raced. Had Evan seen the way Sophia's eyes mirrored his own? That impish tilt of her smile that was all him?

I couldn't believe she had walked up right then. Not that I could be upset with her about it. No, the blame rested squarely on my own shoulders. Well, and Evan's distractingly broad ones.

I had to keep it together. I dodged between families with cotton candy and little kids waving flags. My blouse and skinny jeans suddenly felt too tight, constricting like my carefully compartmentalized life was about to—if Evan made the connection.

Maybe he was stupid.

A girl could dream.

Reaching the solace of a quieter street, off the parade route, I slowed my frenzied pace, gulping down the humid summer air. I glanced back, half-expecting to see Evan's tall figure striding after me, but thankfully, there was no sign of him.

"Hey, Samantha!" Gladys Pinkman waved, her cat-eye glasses slipping down her nose. "Great day for a parade, huh?"

"Absolutely, beautiful as always," I replied, the words mechanically cheerful while my insides churned like butter. I flashed her what I hoped was a convincing smile before continuing on.

I pressed a hand to my chest where my heartbeat still tapped out an SOS. It was just another day in charming Minden; no need to let on that my world threatened to unravel with the mere presence of one man from a spring break long past.

I stress-cleaned our apartment for several hours, even scrubbing the cabinet doors and the base-boards. When the call from Ella's mom came, I carefully scanned the parking lot for any sign of Evan before I went to pick her up.

"Come on, let's get you home," I said, taking Sophia's hand as we left Ella's. Sophia's lips were stained blue from popsicles and her hair was still wet from swimming. The drive home was short, but my mind was far away, every mile chased by thoughts of Evan and his possible suspicions.

"Mom, what are we having for dinner?" Sophia's question pulled me back to reality, even as I felt a rush of gratitude for the mundane task ahead.

"Burgers and chips." I forced cheer into my voice, hoping it sounded more convincing than it felt.

Once inside our kitchen, with its familiar yellow walls and the refrigerator covered in Sophia's school projects, I set about forming the burger patties. Cooking was supposed to be therapeutic, wasn't it? But as I seasoned the burgers and the baked beans began to simmer, my heart refused to settle.

"Can you grab the ketchup, honey?" I asked Sophia, who was setting the table.

"Sure, Mom." She opened the fridge, then paused, her back still to me. "Hey, who was that hot firefighter you were talking to earlier? At the parade?"

The salt shaker slipped from my hand, clattering against the countertop. "Oh, him?" I laughed, a little too loudly. "Just someone from town. I met him when we had that fire at the library I told you about."

"Seemed like he knew you," Sophia persisted, her curiosity as innocent as it was unnerving.

"Knew me?" I repeated, feigning confusion while pressing the George Foreman grill down extra firmly. "Minden's small, sweetheart. Everyone knows everyone."

Sophia seemed to accept this, thankfully moving on to tell me about her day with Ella. She chattered away, filled with a simple joy I envied. If only my own narrative could be rewritten with such ease— free from the hidden chapters that threatened to surface with every mention of Evan Mercer.

We ate dinner and then set up outside on the balcony. The evening sky turned into a canvas of vibrant hues—purples and pinks eventually bleeding into the deepening blue as night fell. Sophia and I settled into our chairs as the citizens of Minden prepared their grand salute to summer and patriotism.

"Look, Mom!" Sophia's delight sliced through my web of worries as the first firework burst into life, a shower of golden sparks raining down upon the town. The air thrummed with the boom that followed, a sound that seemed to echo the persistent pounding in my chest.

"Beautiful," I murmured. As more fireworks

arched skyward, exploding into dazzling arrays of color, my mind betrayed me, spiraling back to spring break in Florida—Evan and I laughing amidst the salty breeze, the sun bronzing our carefree faces, and nights that promised endless possibilities.

"Mom?"

Sophia's voice tugged me back, but not before a wave of resentment washed over me, colliding with the sweet nostalgia of Evan's smile. How easily affection could turn to acrimony.

"Sorry, sweetheart, just lost in thought." A small laugh escaped me, hollow as the flicker of the affection I once felt for Evan. It was there, somewhere, buried under years of self-preservation.

"Are you okay?" Her perceptive eyes searched mine, reflecting the firework-lit sky.

"Of course, just enjoying the show with you." My smile was genuine this time because, despite the turmoil, these moments with her were my sanctuary.

A shiver ran through Sophia, and without a word, I drew her closer to me on the outdoor loveseat. Her small frame leaned back against my chest as the night sky erupted.

"Wow," she breathed out, her voice filled with that pure, untainted wonder only a child can possess.

"They're so cool. How come we don't light any fireworks?"

"Well, mostly because they're expensive. And I'm pretty sure it's against the rules to light them at the apartment complex." I wasn't entirely confident in that, and I could hear someone on the other side of the building shooting some off. But the money thing? Yeah, that was true. Obviously, some people had extra money to literally light on fire and send into the sky, but not us.

"Oh. Okay. At least we can watch everyone else's."

I chuckled lightly, the warmth of her head against my shoulder thawing the cold tendrils of anxiety that had wound around my heart. I was grateful for her easy acceptance of my answer. My arms tightened around her protectively, the action instinctual, as if by holding her close I could shield her from life's harsher realities.

Sophia, my brave girl. At thirteen, she'd already faced more than most adults. It was these moments —the laughter, her curiosity—that fueled my determination to keep her safe, to give her a life as full and vibrant as the fireworks.

The fireworks continued, sporadic across the skyscape as various houses around town lit their own. The lights cast a rainbow glow on Sophia's awestruck face. "Ooh, that one was pretty," she whispered, her small hand gripping mine a little more tightly with each explosion.

I could feel the weight of Evan's gaze from earlier, heavy with questions he hadn't yet asked. What if he put it together? The Mercer family had resources that could easily unearth the secret I'd kept buried for so long, and then rip her from my arms.

I watched Sophia's chest rise and fall in the rhythm of innocent fascination, oblivious to the storm brewing just beyond the horizon of her world. Mercers were known for their ruthlessness in business. If Evan—or worse, his family—discovered Sophia was one of them, what lengths would they go to claim her?

"Did you see that one?" Sophia pointed toward the eastern sky.

"Ooh, purple," I murmured, my response automatic as my thoughts churned. My daughter needed protection; not from the imaginary villains of comic book lore, but from a real threat wrapped in power and prestige. I couldn't let the Mercers swoop in and upend the life we'd built, brick by hard-fought brick.

The secrets I'd carried felt heavier than ever, but

they were mine to bear—for Sophia. For the love that bound us tighter than the tightest knot.

Sophia rested her head against my shoulder, her energy spent from the excitement of the day. I knew she felt safe in my arms, unaware of the storm brewing just beyond our little balcony. As the echoes of the fireworks dwindled as my watch display approached midnight, I closed my eyes and offered up a silent prayer, a plea really, for strength and guidance.

I pleaded with God to help me keep her safe.

My carefully constructed world was trembling beneath the weight of secrets and inevitable confrontations on the horizon. Evan Mercer's unexpected reappearance in my life threatened everything. But I was afraid I was out of options.

CHAPTER 8

Evan

I wasn't sure why I was at the library—to confront Samantha? Demand answers? Maybe just to lay eyes on her again.

But before I could figure it out, I saw someone I hadn't expected.

Sophia.

Curled up in a worn armchair, a book balanced on her knees, completely lost to the world within its pages. Oblivious to me. Oblivious to the storm raging inside my chest.

And just like that, any illusion of control I had vanished.

I searched for any sign of Samantha, but she was nowhere to be found. Which was good, because I was ninety percent sure she would cut me off at the knees before she let me talk to Sophia alone.

"Hey there," I said softly, not wanting to startle the young girl.

Her head popped up, and even though I was a grown man who ran into burning buildings for a living, I found myself hesitating. The way she looked at me then, with that open, warm smile—it was enough to nudge my feet forward.

"Hi. You're Evan, right?" She bookmarked her page with a gentle touch. "From the parade."

"I am. And you're Sophia." She nodded shyly. "Whatcha reading?" I asked as I settled into the chair opposite hers, trying to make myself comfortable without engulfing the entire seat.

"It's a novel about time travel—really fascinating." Her eyes lit up, animated by the topic.

"Time travel, huh? Ever wish you could zip back to certain moments or...?" I trailed off, genuinely curious about her answer.

"Sometimes," she admitted, tilting her head thoughtfully. "But more than going back, I think I'd like to see where things end up. To see if..." She trailed off, her cheeks pinkening. She had that look of someone far older than her thirteen years, like she'd pondered these questions before.

"To see your future," I said, nodding slowly. "Are you sure you want to know? Knowing could be the thing that changes it."

"Exactly! That's what this book is about," she said, lifting it slightly to show me the cover. "Every choice you make sets off a chain reaction. It's kind of cool to think about."

"Sounds pretty deep for a summer read," I said with a grin.

Sophia laughed, the sound light and effortless. "What can I say? I like my vacations with a side of overthinking."

"Can't argue with that," I replied, chuckling.

We fell into a comfortable silence, the kind that wasn't awkward but felt like the pause between paragraphs on a page. I watched her as she fiddled with the edge of her book.

"So," Sophia said, suddenly tilting her head to one side as if struck by a sudden thought, "do you know my mom very well?"

I paused, feeling the weight of years in her simple question. There was a history there, one that hung heavy in my chest. I chose my words carefully. "We were friends a long time ago," I finally replied, the hint of nostalgia creeping into my voice like smoke through closed doors.

"Hmmm." She nodded, seeming to accept the answer. It was disarming, really, how someone so young could possess such poise.

The conversation meandered then, flowing effortlessly from the book she was reading to the odd quirks of life in Minden. As I listened to her speak, the timbre of her voice carried a warmth that tugged at something deep within me. The more we talked, the more I saw fragments of Samantha in her gestures, in the earnestness of her eyes.

The cadence of Sophia's laughter was a melody I never knew I'd missed, but before another word could dance off my tongue, reality came crashing in.

"Excuse me." Samantha's voice was cool and precise. I turned to face her, noting the tightness in her jaw. "Evan, can we talk? In private," she added with a glance toward Sophia.

"Of course," I replied, standing up a little too quickly, the chair screeching in protest against the library's aged wooden floor. I shot Sophia an apologetic smile, which she returned with a curious tilt of her head, and followed Samantha down the narrow aisle between shelves heavy with whispered stories.

As we walked through the maze of bookcases, there was no mistaking the purpose in Samantha's stride. She was ticked.

"Is everything alright?" I ventured, my voice betraying none of the storm brewing within. The librarian in her would appreciate the hushed tone, but the woman who once knew my heart might hear the underlying concern.

"Not here," she said curtly, leading me to a secluded corner of the library before whirling on her heel.

"You shouldn't be here. You can't be talking to my daughter." Her exasperation and anger was written all over her face. And a hint of fear I hated to see. She stood across from me, arms crossed in a barricade I remembered all too well.

Her gaze held mine, searching for an answer or perhaps the resolve to pose a question of her own. And there we stood, two stories intersecting at a crossroads, the next sentence yet unwritten.

I ignored her statements for now.

"Is Sophia just *your* daughter? Or is she mine, too?" The question hung in the air like the motes of dust swirling in a shaft of sunlight filtering through the high windows.

Her reaction was immediate, a sharp intake of breath as if I'd knocked the wind out of her. "What? No," she replied quickly, a crack in her usually composed façade. "Evan, you're not—"

But her words splintered there, and the fragments hung between us, suspended in disbelief. My heart, which had been pounding against its cage, seemed to stop altogether. For more than a week, I'd been turning over the meeting at the parade in my mind. Running the timeline, trying to figure out what it meant. I'd quietly asked everyone I knew in town, which admittedly wasn't very many people, about her. Only to have everyone say the same thing. No one knew who Sophia's father was.

But Samantha was saying it wasn't me.

I looked at her, really looked, trying to find the Samantha I once knew. The one whose laughter could light up the darkest room, and whose honesty was as clear as the depths of her eyes. But this woman before me was shuttered, closed off with walls so thick I couldn't hope to climb them.

"Sam," I said again, softer this time, the name feeling foreign yet achingly familiar on my tongue. "Don't lie to me. Not about this."

My mind raced, piecing together snippets of memories, trying to bridge the years we'd lost. The warmth of her smile, the touch of her hand—it all flooded back, along with the ache of our sudden separation. Jealousy flared within me, unbidden and fierce. Had there been someone else? Another man who'd stepped in so quickly after our fling?

I wanted to shake the truth from her, to wake up from this dream where everything I thought I knew was turned on its head. The silence stretched taut, ready to snap. It took every ounce of strength I had not to let the hurt twist into anger.

"Look at her, Samantha," I urged, my voice low and strained. "She has your eyes, your smile. She's curious and kind and—"

"Stop," she interjected, her voice steel wrapped in velvet. "Just stop, Evan."

But I couldn't stop—not now, not when the possibility of a connection like this dangled just out of reach. My gaze bore into hers, searching for any sign of the truth.

"Tell me," I pressed, my resolve hardening. "Tell me I'm wrong."

The library, with its towering shelves and whispering pages, felt too small suddenly, the weight of our shared history pressing down on me. And as I awaited her response, it wasn't just answers I sought. It was redemption, a second chance at a story I thought had ended long ago.

"You're wrong," she whispered. "She's not yours."

The words hit harder than I expected, a sharp, surprise blow to the ribs. She wasn't mine.

I should have felt relief. I should have walked away, reassured that my past hadn't left a mark I never knew about. But instead, an ache bloomed deep in my chest—raw, inexplicable, and wholly unwelcome.

I swallowed hard, glancing toward Sophia across the library. She was still tucked into her chair, completely unaware of our confrontation. She wasn't mine. That truth should have settled things, but it only left a hollow space where something unnamed had taken root.

"You hesitated," I said, my voice quieter now, less demanding but no less desperate.

Samantha's jaw tightened. "Because I knew you wouldn't believe me."

She was right. I didn't. Not because I thought she was lying, but because something inside me didn't want to accept it. I had somehow come to accept the possibility that Sophia was mine. I had been looking for myself in her—in the way she smiled, in the way she carried herself with quiet confidence. I wanted— what? A connection? A chance to rewrite the past, to make up for what I'd lost?

But there was no fixing what was never broken.

And that was the most frustrating part. If Sophia wasn't mine, then there was no reason for this continued draw toward Sam. She deserved better than me and had obviously moved on from our ill-fated affair.

I exhaled slowly, dragging a hand down my face. "I don't know why this matters so much to me."

Samantha's expression softened, the fight in her eyes flickering for just a moment. "Neither do I."

How had I let so many years slip through my fingers without finding her? If I had been more persistent, if I had pushed harder against the walls she built, could I have been there for Sophia? For Samantha as a young, single mother? Would I have raised another man's child?

I left the library with my head spinning, the echo of Samantha's denial haunting each step.

CHAPTER 9

Samantha

The phone call came when I was reshelving books, my cell phone vibrating urgently in my pocket.

"Mrs. Brown," the camp counselor's voice trembled, "it's about Sophia... she's collapsed. We're not sure why."

I couldn't remember ever moving so fast; one second, I was shelving books on ancient history, and the next, I was bolting for the door, my hands shaking as I clutched the phone to my ear.

"Is she—" I choked out, but the words lodged in my throat, thick with dread.

"Paramedics are on their way. Please come quickly."

Before I knew it, my sensible librarian shoes

were slapping against the pavement, my heart hammering a brutal rhythm that echoed my frantic thoughts. I couldn't lose her. Not my Sophia.

I practically threw myself into the car, fumbling with the keys before the engine roared to life. The streets of Minden blurred past me as I sped toward Bloom's Farm. The world slipped into fast-forward, the quaint shop fronts nothing more than a smudged watercolor streaking by the window, then open fields of farmland.

Twenty minutes felt like an eternity.

"Please be okay, sweetheart," I whispered between clenched teeth, my grip on the steering wheel turning my knuckles white. The air conditioning blasted against my flushed skin, but it did nothing to cool the heat of panic scalding my insides.

"God," I said, not sure if I was praying or bargaining, "just keep her safe. Let her be okay." There was a time when my words to Him were more formal, but today, they tumbled out raw and pleading. I could feel the weight of every silent prayer from the parents who'd ever paced hospital floors, every unwavering hope that things would turn out right.

My mind raced through every memory of Sophia's condition. She had been diagnosed with Long QT Syndrome five years ago. I'd never forget the terrifying moments of pain and dizziness, the relief that came with a promise that we could manage the condition. And yet here I was, again teetering on the edge of every parent's worst nightmare.

The world tipped sideways as I stumbled out of the car, my gaze fixed on the whirlwind of activity that had overtaken the usually tranquil farm. The ambulance was already parked in front of the barn. The sight of worried counselors and campers with faces drawn tight in fear sent an ice-cold shiver down my spine.

"Where is she?" I yelled. My eyes searched frantically for that one face, that one soul who mattered beyond all measure—Sophia.

Evan came toward me. "Sam," he said, his voice steady. "Come with me, she's over here."

"Thank you," I managed, breathless as I followed him to the stretcher. Three additional EMTs surrounded her. The Minden Rogers Fire department had beaten me here. There she was, my little girl, fragile yet fierce even in her stillness. Fear tightened around my throat, threatening to choke me with its cruel grip.

"Stay back, ma'am," another paramedic instructed, not unkindly, but Evan waved him off.

"It's okay, she's the mother," he assured them, and I nearly sobbed in gratitude for his intervention. For a moment, the weight of single parenthood lifted, eased by Evan's protective presence.

"Hey, sweetheart," I whispered to Sophia, reaching out to brush a stray lock from her pale forehead. Her eyelids fluttered, and I took that as a sign—she would fight. She was mine, after all.

"Let's get her to the hospital," Evan said, his tone professional yet tinged with something else—something personal.

"I'm coming with," I stated firmly.

The other firefighter tried to argue. "Ma'am, we can't allow you–"

"I'm coming with," I said again. I'd had this fight before, and just like before, there was no way Sophia was going anywhere without me.

Evan searched my eyes for a moment. He gave a curt nod, and together we moved with the stretcher toward the waiting ambulance. "You can ride shotgun," he said, leaving no room for argument.

I'd take what I could get.

The ambulance doors slammed shut, sealing me inside a cocoon of flashing lights and sterile smells. I clung to the front passenger seat armrest. My gaze flickered to the rearview mirror, where Evan's reflection hovered over Sophia.

"Her vitals are stable for now," he announced, his voice cutting through the hum of the engine and the siren's piercing cry. "Blood pressure is low. Sophia, can you hear me?"

"Mom?" Her voice was weak, a thread of sound winding its way to my ears, fraying my heartstrings with its vulnerability.

"I'm right here, baby," I called back, struggling to keep my tone light. "Evan's taking good care of you."

"Good," she murmured, and I imagined her smile, that tiny curve of lips that always seemed to say, 'I've got this, Mom.'

"Has she ever collapsed like this before? Does she have any pre-existing conditions?"

There it was. I hesitated, the air thickening around me, my fingers tightening around the armrest until my knuckles blanched.

"Sam?" he asked again.

"She has Long QT."

From my peripheral vision, I saw Evan pause, his silhouette rigid against the flicker of red and white lights that bathed the interior of the ambulance in an eerie glow. He leaned closer to the window, his eyes searching mine for something more than just medical information. I held his gaze, feeling the fabric of our shared past stretching taut between us.

I cleared my throat, each syllable an effort. "It's a heart condition–"

"I know what it is," he replied, his tone laced with an undercurrent of something unspoken.

My heart sank. This was what I was afraid of.

Long QT was genetic. When Sophia had been diagnosed, they tested me too. But I didn't carry the gene marker. Which meant she'd gotten it from her father's side of the family. The father who I'd just last week lied to and insisted she wasn't his. It had been a long shot to hope that he wasn't familiar with the condition.

"How long have you known?" he asked, his voice low and controlled, but I could hear the tremor of emotion beneath the surface.

I swallowed hard, my throat suddenly dry. "Since she was eight."

"Five years," he breathed, and I could see the muscles in his jaw tighten.

"Is there anything else we should know?" he asked, though his voice cracked ever so slightly on the last word. His professional mask slipped for a moment, revealing the raw edge of personal shock. It was as if I could see the cogs turning behind those kind eyes of his, piecing together a puzzle whose image he had long suspected but never confirmed.

"She's on a beta-blocker. She hasn't had an episode in over two years."

"Matteo, call the ED and let them know what we've got coming." He turned back to Sophia. "Okay, Sophia. We're going to get you to the doctors okay?"

"Thank you," I whispered, though whether it was for his understanding or his care for Sophia, even I wasn't sure.

"Always," he said, and the simplicity of that word carried a weight of promises, broken and unbroken alike.

The rest of the ride unfolded in silence. Evan busied himself monitoring Sophia, occasionally calling updates to Matteo.

The ambulance doors flew open as if released from an unseen pressure, a pressure that had been building with each revelation and unspoken word between Evan and me. I followed the stretcher, my hand hovering above Sophia's still form. The sterile smell of the emergency room mingled with the sharp tang of antiseptic, grounding me to the moment.

"Stay strong, baby girl," I whispered, more to myself than to Sophia, who was lost in a world between consciousness and the steady beep of monitors.

I risked a glance back at Evan, whose eyes held my gaze with a gravity that seemed to stretch across the expanse of our shared history. There was a tension there, a silent conversation that needed no words yet spoke volumes. It was as if we were both actors in a play we never rehearsed, suddenly aware that the script had changed irrevocably.

CHAPTER 10

Evan

I sat on the steps outside her apartment for what felt like an eternity, my legs beginning to cramp from the awkward perch. My fingers drummed against the concrete, an involuntary response to the tension churning inside me. I couldn't even distract myself with my phone. Every time I tried, I just ended up doing searches about the genetics of Long QT syndrome and how to run a paternity test.

I wasn't leaving until I talked to her though. Jake had done me a solid favor, convincing one of the nurses to give me a heads-up when Samantha was running home. It had taken everything I had to walk away from the emergency room yesterday, and even more restraint to stay away after my shift ended at eight this morning.

As much as my heart was screaming at me to force my way into the hospital room, I knew I couldn't. Not yet.

So instead, I was sweating through my shirt as the unforgiving sun beat down on the apartment entrance. I stared down at my shoes, wondering why the steps I'd taken in life would have led me here. That night hadn't been life-altering enough?

I heard a car door slam and slow footsteps approached. They stopped abruptly. I glanced up and found her standing on the walk a few feet away.

Samantha looked like she hadn't slept in days. Her usually neat hair was a tangled mess, strands falling loosely around her face, some sticking to the faint sheen of sweat on her forehead. Her eyes, normally warm and steady, were bloodshot, with dark circles hanging beneath them, as if the weight of worry had stolen the rest of her energy.

Her clothes were wrinkled, the dress pants and loose cardigan hanging limply on her frame.

But even in her exhaustion, there was something in her posture, a quiet strength that demanded attention. She was fragile, yes, but she was holding it all together. The lines of her face were drawn with fatigue, but there was no denying the fierce protectiveness that radiated from her. She was a mother, through and through.

And she was hurting.

"I can't do this right now," she said, sounding exhausted to the core. I pushed aside the concern for her well-being that needled its way into my thoughts.

"This conversation is not optional," I retorted, unable to keep the edge from my voice. It was as if it had a mind of its own, demanding and urgent, betraying the turmoil that was eating me up inside.

She inhaled sharply, her movements precise as always, but I could see the surprise flicker across her features.

"First of all, how is she?" I asked, gentling my tone as I stood to look her in the eye. I wanted to demand answers, to shake the truth out of Samantha like leaves from an autumn tree, but concern for Sophia held me in check. It was a strange feeling, caring so deeply for someone I barely knew, yet feeling tied to by an invisible thread.

Samantha looked at me, her lips trembling just slightly, but her expression remained closed off. "She's stable," she said quietly. "Just needs to rest. The doctors are monitoring her heart closely."

I nodded, the lump in my throat growing heavier with every word she spoke. She wasn't ready to break—not yet. But I could see it in the way her shoulders sagged when she thought I wasn't looking. Samantha was running on fumes.

I shifted my weight from one foot to the other, trying to find a comfortable stance on the unforgiving concrete steps. The evening breeze carried the scent of freshly mowed grass and the distant hum of a lawn mower, a reminder of normalcy in a world that felt anything but normal.

"I need to know the truth about Sophia." My hands clenched into fists at my sides, as if preparing to fight.

Her eyes dropped to the ground before meeting mine once more. She stood a little straighter, an unconscious preparation for the impact of truths long buried. "Evan," she began, her voice steady despite the tremor I could see in her hands.

"Don't lie to me this time. She's mine, isn't she?"

Part of me was still expecting her to deny it.

Samantha's heart seemed to sink, her shoulders drooping ever so slightly under the weight of the secret she'd carried alone for too long. But then, with a subtle shift, she steeled herself, facing me with a resolve that I couldn't help but admire, even as it tore me apart.

"Seems like you already know she is," she replied, trying to push past me.

Time stood still. The world stopped spinning, or maybe it spun too fast for me to keep up. Words escaped me, as did the breath from my lungs. Fury surged through me like wildfire, burning away the years of detachment I'd cloaked myself in. It was as if I'd been living in black and white, and suddenly the world erupted in unforgiving color.

I bit back a curse word, stepping away from the door and pacing on the short walkway. "How–" I managed to say, my words dissolving into the hot afternoon air. "How could you keep this from me?" My voice broke through the silence, raw and unfiltered. Her admission hung heavy around us, a confession that changed everything, a truth that demanded its due after years of being locked away.

I stared at Samantha, feeling the fury building inside me like a storm brewing on the horizon, as she remained silent. "You stole years from me," I said, my voice rising uncontrollably, each word sharpened by betrayal. "Years I could've had with *my daughter.*"

Holy smokes. The words hit me like a sucker punch. My daughter. Sophia was my daughter.

"I did what I had to do," she insisted, defiance mixing with a hint of regret. Her shoulders squared, even as her voice shook. "I was alone, Evan. I did what was best for her."

"Best for her? Or easiest for you?" I challenged, unable to keep the edge from my words. My heart raced, fueled by a potent cocktail of anger and heartache.

"You weren't here! You never came."

"I tried to find you," I said, each word heavy with the weight of those fruitless efforts. "But you vanished. You could have found me."

Samantha's voice cracked, betraying her fortitude. "I had to make a choice, Evan. And every day, I lived with it, knowing one day this reckoning would come. I was–am–terrified about what you'll do now that you know."

"You made a choice," I muttered, the words tasting bitter on my tongue. As much as I wanted to bridge the gap between us, to understand and forgive, the hurt was too raw, the wound too fresh. "A choice to rob me of our daughter's childhood. What about my choices? What about my right to know, to be there for her?"

"I'm sorry, Evan. I truly am," she said, her voice breaking. She sat down on the step I had vacated.

I took a step forward, a few scattered rocks beneath my boots crunching like a harsh whisper against the backdrop of our raised voices. Samantha squared her shoulders as if bracing against an invisible storm.

"Tell me," I pushed, each word heavy with years of buried emotion. "Why did you hide her from me? What about that week was so terrible that you'd rather Sophia grow up without a father than reach out to me.

"I—I thought..." But her words trailed off, swallowed by the thickening air between us.

"Thought what? That I wouldn't want to be a part of her life? That I'd turn my back on my own daughter?" The accusation tasted bitter on my tongue.

"No, it wasn't like that," she insisted, her voice climbing with every syllable. "I was afraid you'd take her away from me," she cried out, tears and anguish covering her face.

I recoiled at her words and resisted the urge to close the distance between us to wipe away those tears. Her words felt like a slap to the face. She thought I would have taken Sophia away from her?

I shook my head slowly, still feeling sliced open

by her sobs. "You made a baby with me. But you obviously don't know me at all."

She sniffed, still staring at the ground. "Say whatever you want, *Mercer.*"

I felt the dig intended by the use of my last name as though she'd used a shovel.

She continued, "I grew up with a dirt floor, a negative bank balance, and a deep resentment of the wealthy and powerful, because when you're raised on food stamps, it's hard not to see the divide as injustice. So don't tell me that I should have believed that the rich boy who knocked me up in the bathroom before disappearing would suddenly want to coparent with me."

Shame flooded me at her words, and I didn't know how to respond. This situation was so messed up.

I stepped toward her, unable to hold back. I leaned over and tipped her face up to mine, studying her expression. My thumbs traced a path under her eyes, smearing the tears across the dark circles. She shuddered at the touch.

"What are you going to do?" she whispered.

What could I say? That everything was okay? That I wasn't torn apart inside? "I just... I need time,"

I finally managed, the world around me reduced to the echoing sound of my own heartbreak.

I heard the words she whispered as I walked away, though I wasn't sure she was intending me to. "I won't let you take her from me."

CHAPTER 11
Samantha

I t had officially been the longest forty-eight hours of my life. From Sophia's collapse yesterday to a sleepless night by her bedside at the hospital and the interaction this afternoon with Evan at my apartment, I was basically a zombie. Someone must have been praying for supernatural strength or something, because I wasn't sure how I was able to stand, let alone put one foot in front of the other.

The seconds ticked away as I sat in the hospital waiting room. I needed to get back in with Sophia, but I just needed another minute. Once I was with her, I would need to put on a strong face. And right now, I was feeling anything but.

The cushioned chairs and muted colors of the

drab room did nothing to ease the tightness in my chest—a knot wound by the confrontation with Evan. His eyes, usually so calm and sure, had been a storm of hurt, confusion... accusation. I'd seen raw pain there, a father's heartache for the daughter he never knew he had.

I wasn't sure I had ever felt as vulnerable as I did when I admitted the truth to him. My deepest fear that he would somehow use his money and influence to take her. That he–and a judge–would look at me and only see the hungry teenage girl with bony shoulders and greasy hair. The girl I still saw in the mirror when I looked too long.

"Hey, Sam." A nurse's voice broke through my reverie, and I stood, smoothing out my fresh jeans, preparing to face the sterile white of Sophia's hospital room.

"Is she awake?" I asked, the question feeling small and fragile in the vastness of the hospital corridor.

"She's watching TV," the nurse replied with a smile that reached her eyes. "And dozing," she added.

"Thank you," I murmured, taking a deep breath before pushing open the door. The familiar beeping of medical machines greeted me. The antiseptic smell was sharp in my nostrils.

Sophia lay nestled among a fortress of pillows.

Her delicate hands were folded across her stomach, the remote clutched in one hand, the other wrapped around her necklace—a tiny silver heart she'd found buried in my jewelry box several years ago.

"Hey, sweetie," I whispered, drawing closer to the bed, careful not to disturb the wires trailing from under the blanket like cautious snakes. My fingers brushed a stray lock of hair from her forehead.

"Mom?" Her voice, scratchy and groggy with sleep, chased away some of the cold dread coiled inside me. My little girl was so strong.

"Right here," I assured her, offering a smile I hoped looked more convincing than it felt. "Just got back."

"I hope you took a shower." Her attempt at humor was weak but genuine, and it warmed me more than any hospital blanket could.

"As a matter of fact, I did." I chuckled, leaning down to press a kiss to her temple. "I even ate dinner." I didn't share the fact that my "dinner" consisted of half a granola bar and a cheese stick eaten in the car on the way back here after Evan's visit.

"It's okay, Mom," Sophia said, her gaze clear and earnest. "We'll get through this. We always do."

We always do. Her resilience–and the promises

of God—was my anchor, her optimism the light in the darkest of rooms. One thing about hard, scary times? You found out where your hope was. My heart broke for anyone who faced these kinds of situations without the peace of a faith in the Lord.

"Of course, we will," I agreed, my voice steady despite the tremor I felt inside. "What's our verse?"

"So do not fear, for I am with you; do not be dismayed, for I am your God. I will strengthen you and help you; I will uphold you with my righteous right hand," she recited, her smile brightening the sterile room more effectively than any fluorescent bulb.

The door to Sophia's hospital room swung open with a swoosh, breaking the silence that wrapped around us like a shroud. Two doctors entered, their white coats stark against the pale walls, their expressions grave. They both reached for the sanitizer pump by the door and applied it to their hands as they said hello. Another woman trailed behind them.

"We've got to quit meeting like this," the younger doctor added with a sad smile. Dr. Chen had been Sophia's cardiologist since her diagnosis. Her voice was always gentle, but tonight it carried a weight that made my heart sink.

"Yes, please," I managed, my fingers tightening on Sophia's hand.

"You've met Dr. Larson. And this is Sarah, one of our patient advocates."

I nodded in a half-hearted greeting. I didn't know what that meant, but I didn't have the bandwidth to care right now. "How's my girl?" I asked Dr. Chen.

"Sophia's stable for now," Dr. Chen began, pulling up a chair to sit beside us. "But we've reviewed her test results. I'm confident that the episode was a result of the heat and the exertion of the activities at camp."

Guilt flooded me. I'd signed her up for horse camp at Bloom's Farm because she loved horses, yes. But also because I couldn't watch her during the day, and I wasn't ready to leave her alone for that long. I should have been more careful.

Dr. Chen continued. "With Sophia's age and given the severity of this episode, I'm strongly recommending an implantable cardioverter defibrillator."

"An ICD," I repeated, the acronym tasting like metal on my tongue. I had done my research, knew what it meant—the promise of safety it offered. The tiny device would monitor Sophia's heart rhythms and correct them with a small electric shock if there was an arrhythmia.

"Exactly," Dr. Larson confirmed, flipping through a chart. "It's a precautionary measure to prevent sudden cardiac arrest. The device is designed to detect irregular heartbeats and deliver therapy accordingly. I think Sophia is a perfect candidate for the device, and it would greatly increase her ability to partake in normal activities for a teenage girl without fear of repeat episodes."

"Could I play soccer again?" Sophia asked.

My heart broke at her hopeful words. She'd loved playing soccer, but two years ago we'd had to pull her out of the rec league after her last cardiac arrest.

"I think that's quite possible with the ICD, yes. However," Dr. Chen said, hesitating for a moment, "there's an issue with your insurance. They've denied coverage for the device."

I felt the air leave the room—or maybe it was just leaving my lungs—leaving me breathless, grasping for composure. "Denied?" My voice cracked, and I hated how vulnerable it sounded. "But... why?"

"Pre-existing condition clauses," Sarah explained, her tone apologetic. "And the high cost of the device doesn't help."

"Cost shouldn't be a factor when it comes to

saving my daughter's life," I said firmly, though panic clawed at my insides like a caged animal.

"We understand," Dr. Chen assured me. "We're not giving up. We'll appeal the denial, but these things take time. That's why I brought Sarah in here. I wanted you two to meet. She's going to do everything she can to push the insurance company to cover this device."

"Then what are our options if they won't cover it?" I demanded, my mind racing. I'd fight tooth and nail, sell everything I owned if I had to. Nothing mattered more than Sophia's safety.

"We can look into charitable programs or payment plans," Dr. Larson suggested, though his voice held little hope.

"Or fundraising," Dr. Chen added. "Community support can make a big difference."

"Fundraising." The word echoed in my head, bouncing off the walls of fear and landing squarely in the realm of possibility. I was no stranger to hard work, to rallying people together—I did it every day at the library. I could swallow my pride and let people donate.

"Okay," I said, drawing strength from the resolve that filled me. "If that's what it takes, then that's what we'll do."

"I'm really sorry—"

"Leave it to me," I interrupted, my protective instincts surging to the forefront, fierce and unwavering. "I won't let bureaucracy or money stand in the way of my daughter's health."

Dr. Chen smiled, but it didn't quite reach her eyes. "So you know, you're looking at around $50,000 for the initial insertion, and about several thousand each year for follow-up appointments to monitor the device. The batteries last 5-10 years, and replacing them is about $10,000. I'm afraid this isn't a one-time expense."

I blew out a heavy breath, my heart dropping. Fifty grand? I didn't have five grand to my name, let alone fifty. What was I going to do?

"We'll keep fighting the insurance company on your behalf," Sarah said. She was probably trying to be encouraging, but I just felt wrung out. I nodded wordlessly.

Dr. Chen spoke to Sophia. "Until we can get that device, you're going to have to continue to take it easy, Sophia. You've done so well for the last several years. Just keep doing what you've been doing."

Sophia nodded solemnly. I could see the sadness on her face. My eyes drifted to the leads attached to her chest, the ones giving the reassuring lines on the screen by the bed.

"We're going to keep monitoring you overnight, but you're all set to head home tomorrow morning, okay?"

"Thank you," I said, still staring at the steady blip-blip of her heart rate.

As the doctors left, closing the door behind them, I turned back to Sophia.

"Do not be dismayed," I whispered, more to myself than to her. The financial burden felt like a mountain on my chest, but I would climb it, move it, or tunnel through it if I had to. For her, I would do anything.

"It's okay, Mom. I don't have to do horseback riding. Or play soccer," she added with a smile I could tell was forced.

I grabbed her hand. "I know, Soph. I want you to be able to do everything you want to do. And it kills me that money is going to be the thing that stands in your way."

"Don't feel bad," she said, her eyes soft and sweet. So innocent. "I love you," she added.

My heart nearly burst. "I love you too, So So." The nickname slipped out and she rolled her eyes at me. She'd asked me to stop calling her that last winter when she turned thirteen. *I'm not a little girl anymore,* she'd insisted. I held up my hands in surrender. "Sorry, sorry. Old habits," I said, my smile widening. She was still my little girl.

The next day, I sank onto the couch, the familiar creak of its worn springs a comforting reminder that we were home.

"Mom, you're hovering again," Sophia's voice broke through my reverie, laced with that gentle humor that seemed to be her superpower.

"Sorry, sweetie." I smiled, trying to mask the worry that clung to me like a second skin. "I'm just glad you're home."

She was sitting at the kitchen table, surrounded by an array of colorful beads and delicate wires as she crafted yet another friendship bracelet.

"Mom, I know you're worried about the... you know, the ICD thing," Sophia said, her voice dropping to a conspiratorial whisper, as if saying it out loud would make it more real.

"Of course I'm worried. But I'm also determined to give you everything you need," I replied. "We've faced challenges before, haven't we?"

"Like when you single-handedly organized the library's summer reading program after the budget cuts," she offered with a proud grin.

"Exactly." I nodded, bolstered by the memory of that victory. "And we'll get through this too. You and me."

"Team Brown does have a nice ring to it." She laughed softly, returning to her bracelet with renewed vigor. "And hey, if all else fails, we can start a jewelry empire and fund the ICD ourselves."

"Plan B: Operation Bling," I quipped, playing along. It felt good to laugh, even if it was tinged with an edge of desperation.

"Operation Moneybags." Sophia's tone was light, but I could see the fatigue shadowing her features.

"Let's stick to Plan A for now," I said, my voice steady despite the turmoil inside. "But keep those designs coming. Who knows? We might need a fall-back option."

"Always prepared," she teased, threading another bead onto the wire.

"Always," I echoed, watching her work, my heart swelling with pride. This girl, my daughter, was the bravest person I knew. And together, we'd weather whatever storms came our way—be it with medicine or miracles, or maybe just a little bit of both.

CHAPTER 12

Evan

I sat there in my apartment, the kind of place that echoed with its own emptiness. The walls were bare except for a clock that ticked away the silence. In that quiet, I was trying to wrap my head around the fact that I had a daughter—a girl named Sophia whose life had been humming along without me.

"Unbelievable," I muttered to myself, raking a hand through my hair. Anger bubbled up inside me, but it wasn't the hot, fleeting kind. It was heavy, the sort that settles in your bones. Betrayal gnawed at my insides like a relentless pest, and loss... well, the loss was a gaping hole where years of memories should have been.

Fourteen years. I'd been going along with my life

for fourteen years, making decisions with no idea that she was out there.

The streetlamp outside cast a soft glow through the blinds, throwing stripes of light and shadow across the room. It felt like I was sitting in a cage, bars of light trapping me in my turmoil. I couldn't stay seated; it was like the chair itself was made of thorns—every second I spent in it was another prick of pain, another sting of what I'd missed.

Standing up, I shuffled over to the side of my bed. It wasn't every day you found out you were a father. And definitely not every day you found out you were a father to a teenager. I let out a half-hearted chuckle at the thought—humor, after all, was my awkward shield against the world's sucker punches.

Kneeling down beside the bed wasn't something I did often enough, but tonight, I needed something more profound than a long run or a sitcom rerun. I closed my eyes, the darkness behind my lids less suffocating than the one filling my room. I just found out about my daughter, and I was feeling all sorts of things I couldn't even name right then. Maybe God could help me figure out how to be there for her. How to be what she needed when I didn't even know she existed until that day. A sigh escaped me, a surrender of sorts to the chaos inside.

Opening my eyes, I let the dim light wash over me, hoping that with it came the peace I sought—the clarity to navigate this new chapter of my life. With a deep breath, I leaned back on my heels, the determination settling in. Sophia was out there, and I was going to be part of her life. Somehow.

"Lord," I began, the word slipping out into the stillness of my apartment. It felt odd talking to the God who never changed when everything tangible in my life had just shifted on its axis.

"Look, I know I've made plenty of mistakes, but this... this is something else." The words tumbled out as I grappled with the gnawing feeling of unworthiness. My voice broke a bit—I wasn't used to laying my heart out like this, even in private. "I'm angry, yeah, but it's more than that." I was hurting. That was the emotion I didn't want to name, even in my solitude. Sadness felt weak somehow. Anger was safer.

The silence seemed to listen, patient and nonjudgmental.

"Help me get past this bitterness, will You? Because deep down, I think I want to be a part of her life. To be the dad she never had." A shiver ran through me, not from cold but from the fear that maybe I didn't deserve this second chance. "I want to do right by her, somehow."

My plea hung in the air, mingling with the dust motes dancing in the streetlamp's glow. I stayed there a moment longer, seeking solace in the quiet before slowly rising, feeling marginally steadier on my feet as I collapsed into bed.

At the firehouse the following day, the scent of stale coffee lingered like a stubborn fog. I sat at the worn-out table, the cup in my hand more a prop than anything else. The warmth seeped into my fingers, a small comfort against the turmoil that had taken up residence in my chest.

"Hey, Mercer." Nathan's voice cut through my reverie as he pulled up a chair across from me. His eyes were keen, filled with concern that was characteristic of him. He was one of the few guys in the station who had kids.

I grimaced. Turned out we had something in common now.

"Morning," I responded, my tone flat. Even to my own ears, I sounded like a man who'd barely slept, thoughts chasing each other in circles all night.

"Rough night?" he asked, the chair groaning under his weight as he settled in.

"Something like that," I admitted, forcing a half-smile that didn't quite reach my eyes. I took a sip of coffee, letting the bitterness jolt my senses.

Nathan leaned forward, elbows on the table, creating a bridge between us with his steady gaze. "You know you can talk to me, right?"

"Yeah, I know." The gratitude for his presence was genuine, even if I wasn't sure I was ready to spill the whole story.

Nathan's chair scraped against the linoleum as he scooted closer, his brow furrowed in a way that told me he was all in for whatever I had to share.

"I found out... I'm a dad. I have a daughter." The words tumbled out before I could overthink them.

"Wow," he said quickly, clearly taken aback. "That's... wow."

"Feels like I've been sucker-punched." I ran a hand through my hair, the short strands offering no real resistance.

"Soo... Are you going back to Chicago?"

I shook my head, a short laugh escaping. "That's the thing. She's in Minden."

He frowned. "You've only been here like, what, five months?"

"She's thirteen years old. And her mom never told me about her."

"Man, I can't even imagine." Nathan leaned in, his voice steady and sympathetic. "You must be feeling all kinds of angry."

"Understatement of the year," I muttered, staring down into my mug as if it held answers. "But there's more than anger, you know? I'm terrified I'll mess it up. Worried it's too late. I'm ticked at her mom. But I'm also…really upset that I missed so much. How do I even move forward with that kind of obstacle between us?"

"Look," he said, his tone gentle but firm, "God's given you this chance with your daughter for a reason. It's easy to focus on what you've lost. But what you need to do is think about the gift you've been given. A second chance to do things right."

"Second chances, huh?" I mused, rolling the idea around in my mind like one of those smooth pebbles you find by the creek, worn down by years of water rushing over them.

"Exactly." Nathan reached across the table, clapping a hand on my shoulder. "If there is one thing I've learned in the last year, it's that God can take the most hopeless situation and turn it into something that's not just repaired, but entirely unbroken and stronger than before."

"Thanks, Nate." His warmth cut through some of the chill that had settled inside me. "I just hope I'm not too late to be the dad Sophia needs."

"Sophia, hmm? As in, Samantha and Sophia?"

I nodded, pressing my lips into a thin line.

"It's never too late," he assured me with a certainty that felt like sunlight breaking through clouds. "Take it from someone who's been there. You've got this, and you've got a whole community behind you—including me."

"Appreciate it," I said, feeling the first stirrings of hope since the news hit me. Sophia. My daughter. The words sounded foreign but right, like a new song you can't help but hum along to, even if you don't yet know the words.

I stood up from the table, Nathan's words echoing in my ears like the distant siren of an engine call. Second chances—the concept felt as elusive as smoke in my hands, but I had to try. But first, I had something else to take care of.

I found myself tapping the screen with a nervous rhythm, heart hammering as I scrolled through contacts until I landed on a name I hadn't sought in years: Jack Sullivan, private investigator. The guy had a knack for digging up what people worked hard to bury. My family had used him for years, and I knew he was the best. He was also the private investigator who had searched for Samantha all those years ago.

"Jack, it's Evan Mercer," I said, my voice steadier than I felt. "I need your help again."

"Evan?" His tone held a mix of surprise and reluctance. "It's been ages. What is it?"

"Samantha Brown."

He sighed. "Come on, Evan. I thought you'd moved on from... that woman."

"Sometimes, the past doesn't stay where you leave it," I replied, trying to infuse some humor into the tension knotting my chest.

"Look, Evan..." He hesitated, and I could almost hear him rubbing his jaw the way he did when faced with a conundrum. "I told you I couldn't find her. I'm not sure I should get involved in old cases... especially ones like yours."

His words struck a chord, and suspicion curled within me like smoke. Why would he hesitate unless something—or someone—had warned him off?

"I found her, Jack." A laugh escaped. It was crazy

when I really thought about it. Years of looking for her and now I'd stumbled into her small town. Of all the gin joints, right? "I found Samantha. And I'm trying to figure out why you didn't. She was never hiding."

"We looked, Evan. I told you that," he insisted.

"Yeah, well. Apparently, you did a terrible job at it. She went to DePauw University, Jack. Not DePaul. But I've been thinking about it. You still should have been able to find her. It's still Indiana."

"Samantha Brown is a common name, man."

I slammed a fist down on my counter. "I don't give a rip how common it is. You were supposed to *find her.*"

Silence crackled over the line, thick and telling. Jack wasn't usually the type to back down, but I could hear it in the way he hesitated. There was something he wasn't saying.

"You know I did everything I could," he finally said, but the words rang hollow.

"No, I don't know that," I shot back. "I know I gave you every detail I had. I know I paid you well. And I know you—*somehow*—couldn't track down a woman who wasn't even hiding."

Another pause. A sigh. "Evan, you have to drop it."

That was it. That was the confirmation I didn't want but knew was coming.

I clenched my jaw, my grip tightening around the phone. "You got shut down, didn't you?"

More silence.

"Who got to you?" I pressed. "Who made sure I never found her?"

A bitter laugh scraped its way out of my throat. My father. It had to be him. The only person with enough influence to manipulate things behind my back. I never should have used the family PI.

"I can't talk about this," Jack muttered. "I shouldn't have even said—"

"Unbelievable."

"Evan, let it go."

But I couldn't. Because this wasn't just about Samantha. It was about Sophia. About the years I lost. About the fact that someone had made *sure* I'd never find the one girl I had ever given a piece of my heart to. And not just anyone. My own father.

How could he?

The Mercer legacy. That's what it was always about for him. Control. Image. Keeping up appearances while the real fire raged behind closed doors.

The anger was still there, a living thing coiled tight in my chest. But beneath it, something else was taking root. A resolve. An intention. Not to let the sins of the father become the sins of the son. Sophia was out there, a young girl who needed her dad. And I was going to be that for her, even if I had to crawl through the wreckage of my family's making to do it.

CHAPTER 13

Samantha

I tucked the last brightly illustrated book back onto the shelf, children's laughter filling the air of The Minden Public Library's children's area. It was a cute space, but the peeling paint on the walls and the threadbare carpet spoke of a budget stretched too thin. Yet, in that moment, the sound of pure joy managed to lift the weight from my shoulders, if only for a breath or two.

"Did you like the story about Otter and Fox?" I asked, smiling at the sea of small, eager faces gathered around me.

"Yeeeees!" they cheered in unison, their enthusiasm infectious.

"Would you eat that snack that Otter made his sick friend?"

"Nooooo," came the chorus of replies.

I laughed. "Remember, books are treasures that take you on adventures," I told them, my eyes scanning the room, taking in the need for renovation even as I tried to focus on their shining faces. "Make sure to come back next week to hear about the pirate who loved to read!"

As the kids scattered, their guardians offering me grateful nods, I began stacking chairs, my mind already racing with the to-do list that awaited me. That respite was short-lived. Mr. Henley, approached me, his expression serious, brows knitted above rimless glasses.

"Samantha," he began, his tone suggesting yet another item was about to be added to my workload. "I need to talk to you about the renovation funding."

"Of course." I straightened up, slipping back into my professional self. "Did one of the grants come through?"

He shook his head.

"I see," I replied, feeling the pressure settle back onto my shoulders, heavier than before. "So what do you need from me?"

"You've always had a knack for rallying support when it counts. If you want this renovation..." He paused. "It has to be you who makes it happen."

"You want me to get funding for the renovation," I said, pushing past the tightness in my throat, "On my own?"

"We can't let the community down, Samantha," he said with a small smile that didn't quite reach his eyes. "And honestly, if you can't manage to lead a minor project like this... Well, I'm not sure you're the kind of leader this library needs."

"Leader, huh?" I murmured, half to myself, as Mr. Henley walked away. I thought he was supposed to be the leader.

Of course, that would require actual work. And I was pretty sure he was allergic to it.

With everything else on my plate, the idea that I had to get funding for this renovation was laughable. And for him to insinuate my job was on the line if I couldn't do what he hadn't been able to do in ten years? What a jerk.

But then, I'd never been one to back down from a challenge. If it was a champion the library needed, then that's what I'd be.

My phone vibrated in my pocket, and I checked to make sure Mr. Henley was out of sight before I pulled it out. A text message illuminated the screen.

Evan: I want to meet Sophia. Tomorrow.

His words, short and direct, felt more like a

command than a request. My heart raced, and the device in my hand suddenly seemed as heavy as the decision it carried.

I closed my eyes, summoning the strength that had carried me through countless challenges before. "Tomorrow," I echoed, the word hanging in the air like a verdict.

Tomorrow?

I wasn't ready.

But it didn't matter. The time for hiding had passed.

For thirteen years, I'd built a life where it was just Sophia and me. I'd fought through exhaustion, scraped by when money was tight, and carried the weight of every decision alone. I had never let myself wonder what it would be like to have help—to have someone else carry even a fraction of the burden. Because there had been no one.

And now, suddenly, there was.

Evan.

A man who had been absent, not by choice, but by manipulation. A man who had spent years searching for me while I had spent years convincing myself I had done the right thing by keeping him in the dark. Why had God brought Evan to Minden after all these years?

I wasn't just afraid of his involvement—I was kind of angry that it was even an option now. Where had he been when I stayed up nights trying to soothe a fever? When I had to choose between paying for groceries and fixing our car? When Sophia asked, *Why don't I have a dad like the other kids?*

And now, just like that, he wanted to spend time with her.

My stomach twisted. How was she supposed to react? She didn't know him. He was a stranger. Would she be excited? Hurt? Would she resent me for keeping him from her?

I swallowed hard and sank onto the large, stuffed chair I used for story time, my fingers gripping the phone as if it could somehow give me answers. Evan wasn't just passing through Minden. He was *here.* And if I knew anything about him and his family, it was that they didn't back down.

Neither did I.

But this time, I wasn't sure if I was supposed to fight *for* something or *against* it.

My fingers hovered over the keyboard, my mind racing through a dozen ways to respond. I could say no. I could tell him Sophia wasn't ready. But the truth was, *I* wasn't ready.

And I wouldn't let him blindside her before I knew exactly what he wanted.

Samantha: Not happening. We meet first. Just us. Tonight.

I hit send before I could second-guess myself.

The response came almost immediately.

Evan: Where?

I blew out a breath. At least he wasn't arguing.

Samantha: The Bistro. 8 PM.

It was neutral, public, and familiar. And it gave me a few hours to pull myself together.

The coffee shop was quiet when I arrived, the usual evening crowd thinning as closing time crept closer. I spotted Evan immediately through the window. He was sitting at a small booth in the corner, back straight, eyes scanning the room. He looked like a man on a mission.

I squared my shoulders and walked inside.

His gaze locked onto mine the moment I stepped through the door. There was something in his expression—determination, maybe a hint of wariness, but also something deeper. Something I wasn't ready to name.

He gestured to the chair across from him. "Sit?"

I hesitated, then did. "Before we talk about

Sophia, I need to know what you're expecting from this."

His jaw tightened. "I don't know yet."

That answer wasn't good enough. "You don't get to just drop into her life and figure it out as you go, Evan. You weren't there for her, and—"

"You think I don't know that?" His voice was quiet but firm. "You think I don't hate that? I searched for you, Sam. I tried. And now that I know she exists, I'm not just walking away."

I folded my arms. "So what does that mean? Do you want weekends? Holidays? Full custody?" My heart dropped as I voiced all the possibilities I'd been rolling over in my head.

His eyes flashed. "I just want a chance. I want to know my daughter."

The words sent a sharp pang through my chest. Not because they were wrong, but because they were right. Because she *was* his daughter, and no matter how much I had tried to protect her, I couldn't change that fact.

But giving him a chance meant risking everything. And I wasn't sure I was ready for that.

A heavy silence stretched between us, thick with tension. Not just the tension of an argument, but something older, something deeper.

I hated how familiar he still felt. How the rough edge of his voice sent a shiver through me, how I could still pick out the flecks of gold in his eyes beneath the dim café lights. I hated that, after all these years, part of me still remembered the way his touch had felt.

I crossed my arms tighter, like that would somehow protect me from the pull of the past. "This isn't just about you, Evan."

His jaw flexed. "I *know* that."

The intensity in his voice sent a jolt through me. I wasn't sure if it was frustration or something else entirely, something dangerously close to the fire that had burned between us once before.

For a moment, neither of us spoke. The air between us felt charged, humming with something I wasn't ready to name.

I looked away, breaking the spell. "You don't know anything about her," I said, my voice softer now, though no less firm.

"That's why I'm here."

His voice was low, steady. Almost gentle. And I also hated that it made my pulse stutter.

I exhaled sharply. "She's smart. Stubborn. She loves books more than anything, and she hates when people talk down to her just because she's a kid." A small smile tugged at the corner of my lips before I could stop it. "She's got this way of looking at the world, like she's trying to figure out its secrets. Her curiosity is exhausting sometimes," I admitted.

Evan was staring at me, something unreadable in his expression. I realized, too late, how intimately I'd spoken of Sophia—like she was *ours*.

Like we were still *something*.

Heat crept up my neck, and I quickly added, "She's had a good life, Evan. A stable life."

He nodded slowly, his gaze never leaving mine. "I'm not here to take that away from her."

Something in my chest ached at the sincerity in his voice. The familiarity of it. This wasn't fair. He wasn't supposed to make me remember. *We'll build a life together. Can't you see it?*

I forced myself to sit up straighter, to put distance between us where there was none. "Then we take this slow."

Evan inhaled, as if steadying himself, before nodding. But then, as if sensing the shift between us, he leaned back, breaking whatever had just passed between us.

"I can do slow," he agreed, his voice suddenly cooler. "But I won't let you shut me out again."

And just like that, the wall was back up.

He was shutting it down. The chemistry, the connection—whatever had just sparked between us —he was burying it beneath layers of restraint.

And maybe that should have been a relief.

So why did it feel like a loss?

CHAPTER 14

Samantha

The ring of the doorbell sent a flutter through my chest, like a flock of nervous butterflies had taken up residence. I wiped my hands on the kitchen towel before making my way to the front door. Opening it, I found Evan standing there, his presence dwarfing the doorway of our quaint Minden home.

"Hey, Sam," he greeted me with a nod, cool politeness lining his words as if we were mere acquaintances rather than fragments of each other's past.

"Hi, Evan. Come in," I said, stepping aside. My voice was even, betraying none of the turmoil beneath. I led him into the living room where Sophia was curled up on the couch, her eyes brightening at the sight of our guest. I'd tried my best to prepare her for this moment. But how did you really prepare your thirteen-year-old daughter to meet their father for the first time?

"Sophia, this is Evan–your dad. Evan, this is Sophia," I introduced them, careful to watch their exchange.

"It's really nice to meet you, Sophia," Evan said, extending a hand that seemed too large against her petite frame.

"Hi." Her smile was genuine, if a little shy. "I remember you. You're the firefighter."

"That's me," he said. "I'm really glad to hear you're doing okay after that trip to the hospital." No trace of fear or regret shadowed Evan's face, just an open warmth that felt painfully absent when he looked at me.

"Yeah. All good. Especially if I can get that–"

I stepped forward, interrupting her before she shared too much. "Can I get you something to drink, Evan?" When Sophia looked at me, I shook my head in a silent instruction. I didn't want her telling Evan about our money troubles.

He shook his head, his eyes still on Sophia. "No thanks. What were you saying, Sophia?"

"Oh… nothing."

"She just wants to get back to horseback riding again soon," I interjected, hoping my face didn't flush with the lie. Well, it was technically true. Just not what she was going to say. We'd been talking a lot about the ICD and how we could get one.

"I know this is a little sudden, Sophia. But I want you to know that I'm going to be here for you from here on out."

My heart stuttered at the promise, remembering the ones he'd made to me. Made and broken. *You're my dream girl. We'll make this work when we get home. This is more than just a fling. I've never felt like this before. We'll be together forever.*

I quickly excused myself to the kitchen to pull myself together.

"So, Sophia, what do you like to do for fun—besides horseback riding?" Evan asked, drawing her into conversation while they sat at the dining table, within my line of sight but worlds away from where I stood chopping vegetables for the salad.

"I love reading. Oh, and making things. I'm really into friendship bracelets right now," Sophia said, her voice carrying a note of enthusiasm.

"Really? That's cool. Could you show me how to make one?" His tone was warm and curious, an invitation to a world I felt barred from.

"Sure!" Sophia perked up, dashing off to her room for supplies before returning with her plastic box. "You can choose to do a braided bracelet or a beaded bracelet. What do you think?" Soon they were sorting through colorful beads, tying knots and exchanging stories.

"Have you ever saved anyone from a fire?" Sophia's voice, tinged with awe and curiosity, cut through the hum of the kitchen.

I glanced over my shoulder, watching as Evan leaned back in his chair, a thoughtful expression on his face. "Well, there was this one time," he began, his deep voice filling the room. I could see Sophia leaning forward, her hands stilled from their bracelet-making, utterly captivated.

"Tell me everything!" she urged, her eyes wide with anticipation.

Evan chuckled, rubbing the back of his neck. He described how he and his team had responded to a call from an old apartment building engulfed in flames. As he spoke, his hands animatedly painted the scene: the smoke billowing into the dark sky, the heat radiating off the walls, and the sound of sirens echoing in the night.

"Everyone was out, except for an old man on the third floor," Evan continued, his voice dropping to a hush as if sharing a secret. "He was scared, and he didn't want to leave without his cat."

"Did you find it?" Sophia's eyes were glued to him, her lips parted slightly in suspense.

"Yep, hiding under the bed. Scared half to death." Evan's smile was gentle, but there was a glint of pride in his eyes. "We got them both out safe and sound."

"Wow..." Sophia breathed out, the simple word filled with admiration. "Mom, can you pass me the scissors?" she asked, and I delivered them with a smile that didn't quite reach my eyes.

"Thanks!" She returned her focus to Evan, who was fumbling with the strings, a gentle humor lighting up his features. "You're pretty brave, you know," she said.

He smiled softly. "It must run in the family," Evan said, meeting my gaze for a fleeting moment across the room. "I think you're about the bravest person I know."

"I'm just a kid," Sophia replied, twisting the last knot on her bracelet, her fingers dexterous from practice. "Mom says being brave doesn't mean you're not scared, though."

Evan's eyes lingered on me, searching. I shifted uncomfortably, pressing my lips into a thin line.

"She's right. I think your mom's pretty brave, too, actually."

I rolled my eyes, focusing on the sizzle of the pan.

"Yep, she's the bravest person I know," Sophia declared, oblivious to the tension that hummed between us like a live wire.

I watched them laugh together, and it was like observing a scene from another life—one that could have been mine had things been different. I was torn between happiness for Sophia, seeing her connect so effortlessly with someone new, and the sting of my own unresolved feelings for Evan. The way his brow furrowed in concentration as he struggled with the tiny bead in his giant fingers, the easy tilt of his mouth when he smiled—it all clawed at memories I kept locked away.

"Doing okay over there?" Evan asked, his voice pulling me back to the present.

"Fine, just fine," I said, perhaps too quickly. I gripped the spatula a little tighter, wishing it were as simple to hold onto my composure.

"Mom's the best cook," Sophia chimed in, pride evident in her voice.

"Is she now?" Evan glanced in my direction, a polite smile on his lips. "Something smells amazing."

"Thanks," I muttered, focusing on the sizzle of the

meat in the pan, letting it drown out the chatter behind me.

"Look, Evan finished his bracelet!" Sophia held up his creation—a clumsy yet endearing band of interwoven colors.

"Looks great," I said, the praise catching in my throat.

I turned back to the stove, stirring the pasta with more force than necessary. Through Sophia's questions, I was discovering another facet of the man I once thought I knew completely. Why did he choose to run into burning buildings instead of boardrooms? He'd been a business major at the University of Chicago, almost ready to graduate and move on toward his MBA. I took a deep breath, willing my heart rate to slow down, focusing on the rhythmic scraping of the spatula against the pot.

"Okay, dinner's ready," I announced, more to break the spell than anything else. I set the plates down, my movements deliberate, trying not to let the swell of emotions overtake me. "Can you clear off the table, Sophia?"

Sophia cleared the bracelet-making supplies off the table and made room for the three of us. Evan stepped into the kitchen, and suddenly, the small space felt even smaller.

I could sense him behind me, the quiet presence of him a weight against my back. He didn't touch me —he didn't have to. The heat of him, the steady rhythm of his breath, the faint scent of clean soap and smoke—it all pressed in around me, making it hard to think.

"Want me to grab drinks?" His voice was even, controlled.

"Sure," I said, forcing myself to sound just as unaffected. I pointed at the cabinet to my left.

I busied myself at the stove, plating the food and pretending I wasn't hyperaware of him standing so close. Pretending I wasn't remembering the last time we'd shared a space like this—so long ago, in a too-small hotel kitchenette where we'd stolen kisses between bites of takeout.

But that was then.

Now, Evan reached past me to grab a glass from the cupboard, his arm barely brushing mine. The briefest touch, yet it sent a jolt through me. I swallowed hard, gripping the serving spoon tighter than necessary.

He nodded, stepping away as if nothing had happened—as if I wasn't standing there, every nerve ending in my body on high alert. He moved through my kitchen like a man who had everything figured out, utterly composed, every action precise. There was no hesitation in him, no indication that he felt any of what I did.

I envied that.

I turned to find him setting glasses down on the table, his expression perfectly detached. Not cold, exactly, but unreadable. Like he'd drawn a firm line between the past and the present, and I was the only one still tripping over it.

"Thanks," I murmured, clearing my throat as I set the last dish down.

His eyes flickered to mine for the briefest second—then away again. A polite nod, nothing more.

And maybe that should have been a relief.

"Let's eat," I said, offering a smile that didn't quite reach my eyes. As they dug into their meal, I watched them, a silent observer to the bond forming right before me. I watched him effortlessly slip into conversation with Sophia, his laughter low and warm, and something inside me twisted.

He was keeping his distance.

And for reasons I couldn't begin to untangle, that realization stung far more than it should have.

After the plates had been cleared, Evan rose to leave. "I better head out. My shift starts tomorrow morning. Thanks for having me over tonight. I had a lot of fun getting to know you better, Sophia."

Sophia was quiet, her fingers fidgeting with something on the table. Then, in a move that seemed both achingly sweet and unbearably painful, she held out a friendship bracelet toward him.

"Here," she said, her voice soft but steady. "I made this for you."

Evan's face softened as he took the interwoven threads, colors vibrant against his calloused hands. "Thank you," he said solemnly.

My heart splintered a little more with each word. It was just a simple bracelet, but it felt like she was weaving them closer together, stitching a new family tapestry where I was merely a background shade.

"Promise you'll wear it?" Sophia's hopeful eyes met his.

"Every day," he replied, securing it around his wrist.

The door clicked shut behind him, and I was left standing there, the remnants of our shared meal cooling on the counter. Sophia sank back into her chair, her shoulders drooping ever so slightly.

"Mom?" Her voice quivered just enough to betray her upset. "Are you mad?"

"Me? Honey, I should be asking you that." I pulled

a chair up beside her, trying to sound more light-hearted than I felt.

She gave a small shrug, a gesture that carried all the weight of her thirteen years of wisdom and worry. "I'm fine, just... I don't know. Sad, I guess. He's really great, isn't he?"

"I think he really cares about you," I replied, the words tasting bittersweet on my tongue.

"Then why..." She hesitated, biting her lip in that way she did when she was mulling over her words. "Why didn't you tell him about me?"

I pulled her in for a hug, pressing my lips to her hair. "I'm so sorry, sweetheart. I did what I thought was the best thing for us. I wasn't sure how your dad would react to the news. And I wasn't very brave." Admitting you were wrong was always hard, but somehow it felt even harder when you were admitting it to a child.

"Is it wrong if I want to keep seeing him? Will you be mad?" She picked at the frayed edge of the tablecloth, not meeting my eyes.

"Sweetie, if having Evan here makes you happy, then it's the right thing. You deserve all the happiness in the world." My voice was firm, even if my heart was quivering like a leaf in the wind. "I could never be mad at you for wanting to spend time with your dad."

"Thanks, Mom." She finally looked up, her gaze clear and searching. "You deserve to be happy too, you know."

I forced a chuckle, pushing down the surge of emotions her words brought. "Well, my happiness is a work in progress."

"Maybe my dad can be part of that progress?" There was an innocent hope in her voice that made my chest tighten.

"Don't get your hopes up, Soph. He's here for you, okay? Not me."

I WAS AT WORK, with a thousand things to do, but my focus was on Sophia and Evan, two tables over, their heads bowed together over her history homework. It had been three weeks since Evan came over for dinner, and the two of them were finding every excuse to be together. School had just started, and I knew Sophia rarely needed help with her assignments, but I couldn't bring myself to talk her out of it when she asked if she could invite Evan to the library after school.

Evan's voice was low but steady as he pointed to

something in her textbook, his brow furrowed in concentration. Sophia nodded along, tapping her pencil against her chin, the picture of deep thought.

I knew that look. It was the same one she got when she was pretending to struggle with a concept just to keep a conversation going.

"She already knows the answer," I murmured under my breath, shaking my head with a small smile.

It was obvious, the way she leaned in just a little closer, the way she hung on his every word. She wasn't here for the homework—she was here for *him*.

And what startled me most was that he was here for her, too.

I wasn't sure what I had expected from Evan when he first demanded to meet Sophia. Hesitation? Awkwardness? A slow, uncertain dance of trying to figure out his place?

But instead, he had stepped into the role like he had always belonged there.

I watched as Sophia shot him a sly grin. "You're really bad at explaining this, you know."

Evan let out a short laugh, leaning back in his chair. "I am explaining it just fine. You're just messing with me."

Sophia gasped, all mock offense. "Wow. You think I would do that?"

"Yes." His answer was immediate, completely deadpan.

I bit my lip to keep from laughing.

Sophia nudged him with her elbow. "Okay, maybe a little." She flipped the page in her textbook, her smile lingering. "I just like hearing you talk about history. You sound like you care about it."

That surprised him. I could see it in the way his expression shifted, like he wasn't sure how to take the compliment.

"It's important," he said after a pause, his tone gentler now. "The past has a way of shaping us, even when we don't realize it."

Sophia nodded thoughtfully, twirling her pencil between her fingers. "That's kind of deep for a guy who looks like he should be in an action movie, jumping out of burning buildings."

Evan huffed a laugh, shaking his head. "I run *into* burning buildings." He shrugged. "I mean, I guess I've jumped out of one or two."

"Yeah, but you don't have a cool catchphrase when you do it, do you?" She wiggled her eyebrows. "Like, *'Time to turn up the heat'* or *'Looks like things are getting a little too toasty in here.'*"

I snorted from my desk, quickly covering my mouth.

Evan shot me an exasperated look before turning back to Sophia. "No, because I have to focus on *saving lives.* Not sounding like a bad action hero."

Sophia sighed dramatically. "That's a missed opportunity."

"I'll keep that in mind," he said dryly, but his smile lingered.

I should have looked away, should have gotten back to work. But I couldn't. Because in that moment, watching them joke so easily, Evan's eyes alight with laughter, Sophia utterly at ease beside him...

I had never seen her look at anyone the way she looked at him. Like she was *finally* getting something she didn't even know she had been missing. It was effortless, the way they interacted. Natural.

"Your chair is a bit wobbly there, let me just—" Evan bent down, reaching for something under the chair. He popped back up, then gave it another shake to make sure he had fixed it.

"Thanks, " she said, sending him a grateful look that was mirrored by the warmth in his eyes.

"Anytime, kiddo," he replied, his usual careful

composure softened around the edges. "Now, back to the Industrial Revolution."

And there I sat, on the fringes of their world, a silent observer caught between the joy of watching my daughter connect with someone so deeply and the ache of memories that danced just out of reach.

"Thank you so much, Evan. You're like...the best at explaining things," Sophia gushed, her eyes reflecting the overhead lights like twin stars of gratitude.

"I'm just glad I could help. Besides, it's easy when I have such a smart daughter."

Sophia's eyes widened, her cheeks flushing with pleasure.

Evan didn't seem to notice the way my entire body locked up, too caught in the moment, too focused on Sophia's reaction. He had said it so easily, so naturally, like the words had been waiting just beneath the surface, ready to slip free.

Sophia beamed, practically glowing under the weight of his praise. "Well, I *do* try," she said, pretending to buff her nails against her sleeve. "Not everyone can be a history genius like me."

Evan smirked. "Oh, is that what we're calling it?"

"Obviously," she shot back, grinning.

I forced myself to breathe, to swallow past the lump in my throat.

She didn't correct him. She barely hesitated. And the worst part? Neither did he.

I didn't even know if Evan realized what he had said—that he had casually referred to her as *his* daughter, as though it was the most natural thing in the world.

And maybe, for him, it was.

For three weeks now, he had been there. Steady. Present. Sophia had latched onto him in a way I hadn't expected, and now, watching her look at him with so much admiration, I felt an uncomfortable twist of emotions coil in my stomach.

Pride.

Fear.

Possessiveness.

She was mine. She had always been mine. I had been the one awake with her in the middle of the night when she was sick. The one who had packed her lunches, tied her shoes, taught her how to ride a bike. Evan hadn't been there for any of it.

And yet, here he was, effortlessly slipping into a role it had taken me *thirteen years* to grow into.

I forced a smile. "Well, I'm glad you got your homework done, Soph. Maybe now Evan can go rescue someone else from the horrors of eighth-grade history."

Sophia rolled her eyes, grinning. "Yeah, yeah. Thanks again, Evan."

He leaned back in his chair, his gaze flicking to me for the briefest second before he nodded. "Anytime."

And somehow, I knew he meant it.

Which should have been reassuring.

So why did it feel like the ground was shifting beneath me?

"Promise you'll come back again?" Sophia asked, a hopeful lilt in her voice as she began gathering her belongings.

"Of course," Evan answered, his hand lifting to ruffle her hair, a gesture so achingly familiar. "You're not getting rid of me that easily. I'm in this for the long haul, kiddo."

"Good." Sophia beamed, her satisfaction simple and pure.

"Ready to go, Mom?" Sophia's voice, bright and expectant, pulled me forward.

Stepping out of the Minden Public Library, the evening air warmed my cheeks, a reminder that although autumn was on its heels, summer hadn't quite loosened its grip. Sophia matched her steps with mine, her shoulder occasionally bumping against mine in that easy rhythm we'd always shared.

"Mom?" Her voice was a timid intrusion into the quiet that had settled between us.

"Hmm?" I glanced down at her, caught off guard by the intensity in her gaze.

"Do you think you and Dad will ever be... friends?" The way she tucked a loose strand of hair behind her ear, a simple gesture marred by hesitation, told me this question had been weighing on her mind far longer than just this moment.

"Friends?" I echoed, stalling for time as my heart did a precarious dance.

I wanted to brush the question aside, to laugh it off with a quip about how adults have complicated friendships. But this was Sophia, her perceptive eyes searching mine for something I wasn't sure I could promise.

"Friendship would be... complicated," I started, trying to keep my tone light despite the tightness in my chest.

"Mom?"

"Yes, sweetheart?"

"Even if you're not friends... you both love me, right? That part's not complicated?" Her question was earnest, seeking assurance in the one constant she hoped remained untouched by the complication of grown-up feelings.

"Absolutely," I responded without hesitation, my voice firm and unwavering. "That's the simplest thing in the world."

Reaching out, I took her hand in mine, squeezing it gently to punctuate my words. Our bond, at least, was something I never had to question, even when everything else felt uncertain.

As we walked on, the library fading into the distance behind us, I allowed myself to feel the full weight of Sophia's question, and my carefully crafted defenses began to crumble. Maybe it was time to face the truth that my heart knew all along: Evan Mercer still held a piece of it, whether I liked it or not.

"Do you think... I mean, would it be weird if I asked him if I could call him Dad?"

The question hung in the air, fragile and weighted, like a dandelion seed caught on a breeze. I felt the sidewalk tilt slightly, my pulse tapping a staccato rhythm against my throat.

I had prepared myself for a lot of things when Evan Mercer crashed back into our lives.

But not this. Not the quiet, tentative way Sophia asked the question. Not the way her fingers twisted in the hem of her hoodie, a nervous habit I'd seen a hundred times before.

I forced myself to breathe, to think, even as my heart squeezed painfully in my chest.

Would it be weird? Maybe.

Would it hurt? Absolutely.

But this wasn't about me.

I swallowed, choosing my words carefully. "I think... that's a big question, sweetheart."

Sophia nodded, staring down at her sneakers. "I know."

I reached out, tucking a loose strand of hair behind her ear. "And I think it's one you should ask him when you're ready."

Her head jerked up. "You don't think he'd be mad?"

"Mad?" My chest tightened. "Oh, honey. No. I don't think he'd be mad at all."

He'd be stunned, maybe. Overwhelmed. I couldn't even imagine what would flicker through his eyes if she asked him something like that.

But he wouldn't be mad.

I had seen the way he looked at her, the way he leaned in when she talked, like every word mattered. Like he was *already* stepping into something bigger than either of us had anticipated.

Sophia let out a breath, her shoulders relaxing just a little. "Okay."

We walked the rest of the way home in silence, her mind clearly turning over the idea, mine desperately trying to prepare for whatever came next.

CHAPTER 15
Evan

As I pulled up to the sprawling estate of my parents' house in Chicago, my heart knocked around my chest like a rookie firefighter facing his first blaze. The place hadn't changed one bit—same intimidating iron gates, same meticulously trimmed hedges that would probably snip themselves out of sheer respect for my father's strict standards.

"Welcome back, Mr. Mercer," said James, the butler who'd been with us since I was knee-high to a fire hydrant. "I didn't have your visit on the schedule today." He always said schedule with a soft "sh" sound that made me smile.

"Thanks, James." My voice sounded steadier than I felt. "It was a spur-of-the-moment visit," I said. The door swung open, and the smell hit me—the rich blend of polished wood and leather that was as much a part of this house as the stone it was built from. Memories flooded back of Mason and me, tearing through these halls, our laughter echoing off the high ceilings. A simpler time, before life got complicated by things like grief and threats to be disowned by my father. "I assume he's in his office?"

"I'll let him know you're here," James said.

"That's okay. I'll announce myself." I wanted to catch my father off guard. It was the only way to get a read on him. We reached the heavy oak door, and James gave me a nod before turning back.

"Good luck," he whispered, leaving me standing there, feeling like I was about to walk into the lion's den armed with nothing but a water pistol.

Taking a deep breath, I pushed the door open. Dad sat behind his massive mahogany desk that looked like it could double as a Viking ship if you flipped it over. He glanced up, barely a hint of surprise flickering across his features. He acknowledged me with a nod so cool it could frost glass.

"Evan."

"Father." I stepped inside, the plush carpet swallowing the sound of my footsteps. It was just like him to create an environment where even your own presence felt muted.

I squared my shoulders, trying to shake off the anxiety. This was it, no backing down now. "We need to talk," I said, my voice steady despite the storm brewing in my gut.

He didn't respond, just shuffled a stack of papers with the detachment of a man sorting through junk mail. But I could see the lines of tension at the corners of his eyes. He knew what was coming. He always knew.

"How could you?" I blurted out, not bothering with the niceties of small talk that had never really bridged the gap between us. My words hung in the air.

He didn't flinch, didn't give me the satisfaction of seeing him react. Instead, he leaned back in his chair, the very image of self-assurance so polished it could reflect his own smugness. "I've no idea what you're talking about," he said, but the flicker of awareness in his eyes told me everything I needed to know.

"Samantha Brown." My voice was more controlled than I felt. The old leather of the armchair creaked under his shifting weight, a familiar soundtrack to countless one-sided conversations.

"Who?"

A rage unlike any I had felt before roared to life

in my chest. His denial wasn't just a lie—it was an insult.

"You *know* who," I ground out, my hands curling into fists at my sides. "Don't play games with me."

Dad exhaled, long and slow, as if he were tolerating an unruly employee rather than his own son. "Evan, if this is about some woman from your past—"

"She's not *some woman*." My voice came sharp and fast, slicing through his feigned indifference. "She's the mother of my child."

For the first time, something flickered across his face—shock, maybe. Or maybe it was calculation, adjusting the pieces of whatever game he was playing.

But he recovered quickly. "And what, exactly, do you think I had to do with her?"

I took a step closer, bracing my hands against the edge of his desk. "You tell me," I challenged. "I hired Jack to find her fourteen years ago. He came up with nothing. Said she disappeared. But she didn't. She was in *Indiana,* Dad. Not some remote island. Not off the grid. You expect me to believe our seasoned investigator just... failed?"

Dad leaned forward, steepling his fingers. "Careful, Evan. Accusations like that—"

"Cut the act." My pulse thundered in my ears. "Did you interfere?"

Silence.

It stretched between us, thick with years of power plays I'd been too blind to see before.

And then, the smallest twitch of his lips. Not a smile—more like the ghost of satisfaction.

"You were never meant for that life," he said smoothly. "She wasn't the kind of woman you needed. You're a Mercer, for crying out loud. I couldn't have you gallivanting around with some two-bit trailer trash–"

"Enough!" I roared. I had never been so tempted to strike my father as I was at that moment. But to hear him talk about Samantha that way? I couldn't.

"Did you know? Did you know about Sophia?"

Before he could answer, the door opened and Mom stepped in, her eyes wide with surprise. "Evan, darling, what's going on?" she asked, glancing between the two of us, her concern etched in the gentle lines around her eyes.

"Nothing to worry about, Elaine." Dad dismissed her with a wave of his hand as if swatting away a pesky fly. She hovered by the bookshelves, unwilling to push him further, but not ready to leave the room.

A quiet, obedient little mouse. Like she'd always been.

"Actually, Mom, there's plenty to worry about." I turned back to face him. "Daddy dearest here still seems to think he can control every aspect of my life."

"Control?" He laughed lightly, the sound hollow in the expanse of the office. "I was trying to save you from a life filled with regret, son."

My jaw tightened as I struggled to keep my emotions in check. The word 'regret' sat heavy in the air, like a challenge. A life of regret? As if he had any idea about the things that haunted me, keeping me up at night, or driving me to run into burning buildings to save strangers because I couldn't save—

"Save me?" I managed to choke out. "By dictating my choices? By hiding the truth?"

"Choices lead to consequences," he said, his voice dipped in the cool, detached tone of a CEO rather than a father. "I was merely trying to guide you towards the right ones."

"Guide?" I repeated incredulously. "You could have cost me the chance to be a father to that little girl."

My mother gave a startled gasp.

"Enough, Evan," my father warned, his indifference slipping just enough to reveal the iron will beneath.

I studied him for a moment—the man who taught me to tie a tie, to ride a bike, and then later, how to hide any vulnerability behind a veneer of confidence. But I wasn't that little boy anymore, running through these halls, seeking his approval. I was a man with calloused hands and a heart that'd been through the wringer. And I'd stopped letting him steer my course fourteen years ago when Mason died.

"Evan, you're too close to this situation. You can't see—"

"No, Dad," I interrupted, my tone leaving no room for debate. "I see perfectly clearly. You've always had this...this script for how my life should go. But I stopped following it a long time ago. Whatever foolish hopes you had for me to leave the fire department behind and take up the family business? That's never happening." The words felt like boulders rolling off my tongue, heavy but freeing.

He let out a derisive chuckle, the sound echoing off the high ceilings adorned with ornate crown molding—the gilded cage of my upbringing. "It's time to move past this little teenage rebellion. Grow up, Evan."

"Rebellion?" I repeated, a mirthless laugh escaping me. "I'm no teenager, Dad. I'm a grown man, apparently a father myself. This isn't about rebelling; it's about living my life, making my choices. And I won't apologize for that."

"Choices have consequences," he said again, eyes narrowing slightly. "And I've always been here to mitigate them for you."

"You've been mitigating them," I echoed, feeling the absurdity of the word in this context. "We're talking about *my daughter*. I already know the weight of my decisions. I carry them every day, on every call. And now, I carry them in every moment I spend with Samantha and Sophia. My choices are mine to bear, not yours to manage."

"You're my son, and I will *not* let you stain the Mercer name!"

A scornful laugh fell from my lips. "We're. Done," I said, feeling each word vibrate through the air, a solemn drumbeat to mark the end of an era. "As far as I am concerned, I am no longer your son. You stay away from me and my family."

I turned on my heel and marched out of the office, only slightly aware that my mother followed me.

"Evan. Evan, sweetheart," she pleaded as she chased me down the hallway.

My heart was racing, my muscles stiff from clenching my jaw and fists. When we reached the foyer, I turned and my mother almost ran into me.

"Did you know?" I stared at her, studying every muted emotion on her overly-botoxed face.

Her gaze softened slightly, and she moved closer, placing her hand on my arm—a touch that used to comfort me as a boy. "I didn't know, I swear," she said gently. "Whatever your father has done, I had no part in it. And... I would very much like to meet your Sophia. My... granddaughter? Please believe me," she begged.

The sincerity in her voice tugged at something deep within me, and I found myself recalling count-less childhood moments when she'd been the buffer between Dad's stern discipline and my own stub-born streak.

"Mom, I... I believe you." The words came out more tenderly than I expected. "And Sophia—she's amazing. You'd love her. She's smart and sassy and has this ability to just... light up a room, even though she's had her share of challenges."

My mother's face brightened at the description. "She sounds like a remarkable young lady."

"Yeah, she is." I felt a smile breaking through despite the emotional whirlwind. "I can't promise anything right now, but I'll think about it."

"Thank you, Evan," she said, her voice carrying years of warmth and a hint of hope that hadn't been there a moment ago.

And with that, I turned my back on the imposing silhouette of the Mercer family home, feeling the last chains of expectation fall away. With a final glance at the Chicago skyline, I started the engine of my well-worn truck. It stood out like a sore thumb amidst the luxury cars of the family driveway. It felt good to leave in something that was unmistakably mine, a symbol of the hard-earned life I'd built. The road stretched out before me, leading back to Minden, back to Sophia. And Samantha.

I'd spent weeks—months, really—fighting against the resentment, the betrayal of what Sam had kept from me. And yet, somewhere between late-night tutoring sessions with Sophia, stolen glances across the library, and the cautious, guarded conversations we'd had, something had shifted.

I didn't just see her as the girl who disappeared. Or the woman who kept my daughter from me.

I saw the mother who had raised Sophia into the brilliant, thoughtful kid she was. The woman who had built a life for them from nothing. Who had protected our daughter, even when she had no one protecting her.

Samantha wasn't my enemy. And that realization felt more dangerous than anything else.

Because if I let go of my anger, if I let myself truly see her for who she was now, then I'd have to admit the truth.

That I still wanted her. Not just because of Sophia. Not just because of the history we shared.

But because she was Samantha. And for reasons I couldn't fully explain, I had never really stopped wanting her.

The thought made my grip tighten on the wheel.

I needed to be here for Sophia. That was it.

And if there was one thing I knew how to do, it was control myself.

I had spent years perfecting the art of shutting things down before they had the chance to hurt me.

So whatever this was—whatever pull I still felt toward Samantha—I would bury it.

The past had shaped my perspective, drilling into me the belief that nothing good came from wanting something I was never meant to have.

And that was the thought I couldn't shake.

I told myself it didn't matter, that whatever

existed between us all those years ago was long gone. That the only thing tethering us together now was Sophia.

But sometimes, when I caught her watching me —when her gaze lingered just a little too long before she looked away—I wondered.

When our hands brushed as we passed each other in her too-small kitchen, when her breath hitched the slightest bit before she turned to busy herself with something else, I wondered.

And when she smiled at Sophia with all the warmth and love in the world, only to glance at me with something unreadable in her eyes, I wondered.

Did she feel it too?

That pull. That connection neither of us had asked for but couldn't seem to sever completely.

I should have let it go.

But even as I told myself to push it aside, to bury it like I'd buried everything else, I knew one thing for certain.

If Samantha felt even a fraction of what I did, ignoring it would be impossible.

And maybe I wasn't the only one fighting a battle I had no hope of winning.

CHAPTER 16

Samantha

The popcorn kernels rattled in the pot, and I stirred them absentmindedly, watching as they jumped and popped. It was almost funny—how something small and hard could transform under the right conditions.

Maybe I needed to do the same.

I wasn't sure when it had happened, but the anger I'd held onto for so long—at Evan for disappearing, at myself for ever believing I could keep Sophia a secret—was starting to feel... exhausting. I had always been able to rationalize my decision to keep her to myself, because he hadn't tried to find me, either. I wasn't hiding her, per se.

But when he'd admitted to trying to find me? I

could feel the little chink in the armor I'd so faith-
fully donned for fourteen years.

It had been easier when he was just a ghost from
my past, but now he was here, a steady presence in
Sophia's life. And despite every instinct telling me to
keep my guard up, I didn't *want* to be angry
anymore.

And moments like these made it all the harder.

"Mom, is it ready yet?" Sophia's voice, impatient
but excited, pulled me back to the moment. "What
flavor are you doing?"

"Almost," I said, giving the pot one last shake. "It's
white cheddar tonight. Will you get the movie
ready?"

She darted off, and I took a deep breath, pouring
the popcorn into a bowl and spraying it with olive
oil. I added the powdered cheese and gave the whole
bowl a few big swirls. Then, squaring my shoulders,
I walked into the living room.

Evan and Sophia were already settled on the
couch, flipping through movie options. They were at
ease with each other, and that alone made my chest
tighten—not with resentment, but something
quieter. Something I wasn't quite ready to name.

"Perfect timing." Evan glanced up, a hint of a

smile tugging at his lips. "What are we watching tonight?"

I hesitated for only a second before sitting down next to Sophia, forcing myself to relax.

Maybe I wasn't ready to let go of the past entirely. But tonight, I could try.

"Something with action, I hope," I mused, handing him the bowl before settling down beside them. I didn't think I could handle anything too romantic.

"Action it is." He smiled, and there was that humor in his eyes that always seemed to make the room brighter. "Let's see if we can find something that won't have us covering Sophia's eyes."

"Hey, I'm thirteen, not three," Sophia protested playfully, grabbing a handful of popcorn. "I can handle action." She yawned through the last several words, and I met Evan's glance over her head. It was already after eight on Friday night, but I'd foolishly agreed to a movie before dinner took twice as long as I'd expected.

We settled on a spy movie with good reviews. With a click of the remote, the movie started, its opening credits rolling across the screen. The room was bathed in flickering light. I nestled closer to Sophia.

About ninety minutes later, the movie had reached the climax, but Sophia's breathing had taken on the deep and even rhythm that signaled she'd drifted off to dreamland. Her head, hair in a messy bun, rested against my shoulder. I glanced down at her peaceful face, feeling a surge of love for this tiny person who had weathered life's storms right by my side.

Carefully, I reached over and pulled the fleece blanket up around her chin, tucking it gently under her arms. She murmured something unintelligible and snuggled deeper into the warmth. I smiled. There's something about a sleeping child that just made the world seem right, even if just for a moment.

With the room now quiet except for the quiet dialogue of the film, I turned my attention back to the screen. But not for long. My gaze was drawn to Evan, his profile illuminated by the TV's glow. He caught me looking.

"Maybe I should go," he whispered, motioning toward Sophia. "Don't want to wake her."

I shook my head, a little too eagerly. "You can stay. It's… kind of nice." The words hung in the air between us, simple but heavy with meaning.

"Alright," Evan said, settling back into the couch.

His presence filled the space with a comforting energy that I hadn't realized I'd missed until just then.

"Thanks for coming tonight, Evan," I continued, my voice a murmur matching the tranquility of the room. "I'm sure there are other things you could do on a Friday night as a single guy."

He offered a half-smile, the kind that didn't quite reach the eyes but still managed to convey warmth. "There's nowhere else I'd rather be."

I let myself ask the question that had been on my mind since I first saw him at the Spring Sparks Auction. "How did you end up in Minden anyway? We're a long way from Chicago."

His lips lifted in a half-smile. "Well, I'm starting to think it was all a God thing, you know. If I hadn't moved here, I might never have found you."

I responded with a low hum, not sure how else to respond.

"I'd been with the Chicago Fire Department for about ten years. I moved up through the ranks quickly, and I was in line for a promotion to a station chief, which is a pretty big deal. But I knew that part of the reason I was even in the conversation was because I was a Mercer. I hated the idea that I was getting something I hadn't earned. So I started looking outside Chicago. When I saw the posting that MRFD was looking for an assistant chief, I decided to apply." He shrugged. "It's worked out so far, I guess."

I shook my head. "That's crazy. Whatever happened to getting your MBA? When we were in Florida, all you talked about was what you were going to change when you took over your dad's business."

His eyes flashed with an expression I couldn't name.

"You know my brother had Long QT?"

I frowned at the change of subject, but shook my head. "No, I didn't."

I turned my body toward him, folding my legs beneath me on the couch. Sophia's steady breathing was a comforting rhythm in the quiet room. I nodded for him to continue, my heart already bracing for the weight of his words.

"That was how I knew so much about it when we picked up Sophia that day. I didn't know until later, but that was what killed him in the fire." His eyes locked onto mine, a raw vulnerability shining through. "He didn't stand a chance, not with the crowd, the smoke... And his heart just couldn't take it."

My own heart dropped at the revelation. "I'm so sorry," I said.

"After his funeral, I decided to join the fire service. Mason was a better person than me, by far. And I just... I wanted to do something that would make him proud. I decided that adding a few zeroes to the family bank account wasn't really all that noble."

I gripped the blanket a little tighter around Sophia, feeling a surge of protectiveness for both my daughter and the man beside me who had suffered so much loss.

"That's why you became a firefighter?" My voice was barely above a whisper, but it carried all the admiration and sorrow I felt for him in that moment.

Evan nodded, a shadow of a smile flickering across his face. "Yeah. I think I thought, if I could save someone else's brother, maybe it would..." His voice trailed off, leaving the sentence unfinished, but I understood.

My heart ached for him, for the burden of guilt he'd shouldered all these years. Watching him closely, I saw the strain in the set of his jaw, the way his hands clasped and unclasped as though trying to release something intangible.

"Evan," I began, my tone deliberate, choosing each word as if it were a lifeline I was offering him. "You didn't let your brother down."

His gaze wavered, a storm of doubt and sorrow threatening to spill over. The silence stretched between us. "I wish I could believe that," he said.

The glow from the television painted his face in shades of blue and gold, highlighting the creases etched around his eyes—lines that spoke of smiles now rare and frowns all too common. In the shifting light, I saw a glimmer of the boy I remembered, the one who laughed easily and dreamed boldly before life demanded a sacrifice he was never prepared to give.

"Sometimes," I said, my voice barely above a whisper, "the hardest person to forgive is yourself."

Evan let out a breath, long and slow, his eyes locked on the screen but clearly not seeing it. The weight of his pain was almost tangible, stretching between us like a thread frayed thin with time.

Between us, Sophia stirred, nestling deeper into the couch cushions, her tiny hand curling instinctively around the fabric of Evan's sleeve. He glanced down at her, his features softening in a way that made something shift inside me.

"She trusts you," I murmured, my voice barely

louder than the hum of the television. "She's comfortable with you."

His fingers twitched, but he didn't pull away from her grasp. "I don't know if I deserve that."

The honesty in his voice wrapped around me, tugging me closer in a way I hadn't expected. This man—this strong, steady firefighter who had walked back into our lives—was still carrying so much guilt. But I saw the way he looked at Sophia, the way he showed up for her, the way he tried. Maybe it wasn't about deserving. Maybe it was about being willing.

And Evan was willing.

That scared me.

For so long, it had been just Sophia and me. I'd built our life on the certainty that no one else would swoop in and change things. I'd been both her safety net and her only constant. But now, here he was, showing up in ways I hadn't let myself believe he ever would.

The weight of his presence wasn't just in the room—it was in my heart, pressing against every wall I'd put up.

I cleared my throat and glanced down at Sophia, her small fingers still curled loosely around Evan's sleeve. She trusted him, but more than that—she already cared about him. The thought sent a sharp pang through me.

If she got attached and he left…

No. I couldn't go there.

Evan shifted beside me, his arm resting along the back of the couch. Not quite touching me, but close enough that the warmth of him sent an awareness prickling across my skin. I tried to ignore it, tried to focus on the movie, on Sophia, on anything but the man beside me.

"She's amazing, you know," he murmured.

I turned my head slightly, just enough to see the adoring look in his eyes as he watched our daughter sleep.

"I know," I said, my voice quieter than I meant for it to be.

He exhaled, his fingers flexing where they rested against the couch. "I hate that I missed so much. I don't know how to make up for it."

I hesitated, searching for the right words. "You can't get back the years we lost, Evan. But you can be here now."

His gaze lifted to mine, searching, questioning. I could see the self-doubt, the hesitation that had nothing to do with whether or not he wanted to be here, but whether or not I'd let him.

I swallowed, knowing I had to take the hit to my own pride to reassure him. "And so far... you're doing great."

Something shifted in his expression.

And for the first time since he walked back into our lives, I realized that maybe I wasn't just afraid of him leaving.

Maybe I was afraid of what it would mean if he stayed.

CHAPTER 17

Evan

The chief was mid-sentence about the new fire engine we were considering when my phone buzzed in my pocket. I slipped it out enough to see Sam's name on the screen. "Sorry, Chief, I've got to take this," I said, already thumbing the screen to life.

"Hey, Sam, what's up?" I stepped away from the chief's desk, the background noise of the firehouse fading as I focused on the silence on the other end of the line.

"Hey... I—" A sigh. Then nothing.

I frowned. "Sam?"

"Never mind." The words came fast, like she was trying to shove them back in before I could catch them. "I'll figure something out."

That set off every alarm in my head. "Hold on. What do you need?"

Another pause. I could practically hear her grinding her teeth. "I hate to ask, but I'm stuck at work. Mr. Henley is on some terror about missing books and insisting we track every one down. Is there any way you could pick Sophia up from school?"

"I thought she took the bus?"

"She had a theatre club meeting and didn't take the bus," she explained. "If there was anyone else..."

While I didn't love that I was her last resort, I wouldn't pass up an opportunity to be there for my girl.

I glanced at the clock. "Yeah, of course. I'll head there now."

Another pause. A quiet exhale. Then, "Are you sure? I don't want to—"

"Sam." My voice was firm, cutting off whatever excuse she was about to make. "I've got it."

Silence stretched for a beat. Then, so quietly I almost didn't hear it, "Thanks. I'll send a message to her watch and let her know."

And then the line went dead.

I tossed a quick salute to the chief, who just

shook his head with a knowing grin, and made my way to the parking lot.

Pulling up outside the school, I parked under a canopy of trees whose leaves were starting to tinge gold. It was already late September, and summer was giving way to fall. I leaned against the car, trying to seem casual, but my heart ticked up a notch, just like it always did.

"Hey, Sophia." I pushed off from the car and offered her the best smile I could muster, hoping to mask the nerves that seemed out of place on a seasoned firefighter. But then again, this wasn't a fire I was facing—it was something far more unpredictable.

Sophia's backpack bounced against her as she made a beeline for me, a grin spreading across her face that could outshine the sun. "Evan!" she exclaimed.

"Hey there," I replied, scooping her into a hug that lifted her feet clear off the ground. She laughed, and I felt the day's weight lift off my shoulders.

"I was so happy when Mom said you were picking me up!" She wriggled free and skipped ahead to the passenger side of my truck.

I blinked, still standing there for a beat longer

than I should have. She was happy I was here. Not just okay with it—happy.

By the time I snapped out of it, she was already yanking the door handle, her energy vibrating in the air around her. I jogged ahead to open it for her, earning a grin that made my chest tighten in a way I wasn't prepared for.

"Buckle up," I said, ruffling her hair as she climbed in. As I did, I wondered if her teenage self would bristle at the affection, but her smile only widened.

She did, chattering away as I slid behind the wheel. I caught Sophia's eyes in the rearview mirror.

"Guess what we did in science today?" she asked, her voice buzzing with excitement as we pulled away from the school.

"Tell me," I said, keeping one eye on the road and another on her animated expression.

"We dissected frogs!" Her nose wrinkled in mock disgust, but the gleam in her eye told me she'd loved every second of it.

"Ah, the rite of passage for all young scholars," I quipped. "Did you name yours before or after the... procedure?"

"Before, obviously." She rolled her eyes with perfect teenage dramatic flair. "His name was

Prince Charming. Didn't turn into a human, though."

"Maybe he was just waiting for the right princess," I teased, and her laughter filled the car like music.

"Or the right scientist," she countered, always quick on the draw.

The chatter continued as we pulled into Samantha's parking lot, the engine ticking softly in the quiet aftermath of our ride. Sophia was mid-sentence, detailing the latest classroom drama with the enthusiasm of a talk show host.

"…and then Kayla said that she wasn't going to speak to Jess anymore, but by lunchtime, they were sharing chips like nothing happened."

"Ah, the politics of seventh grade," I mused, parking the car and killing the engine.

Sophia giggled, gathering her backpack as I stepped out of the car.

"Thanks for picking me up, Evan," she said, slinging an arm around my waist as we walked toward the apartment.

I rested my hand on her shoulder, giving it a small squeeze as we reached the door. "Anytime, kiddo."

She fished her key out of her backpack and

worked it into the lock with the confidence of someone who'd done it a hundred times before. As the door swung open, she flicked on the lights and tossed her backpack onto the couch in one fluid motion.

"Are you staying for a bit?" she asked casually, kicking off her shoes and heading toward the kitchen.

I hesitated. I hadn't planned on it. But something about the way she asked made it impossible to just turn around and leave.

"You good here by yourself?" I asked instead, eyeing the empty apartment.

Sophia rolled her eyes as if I'd just asked if she still believed in Santa. "Mom lets me stay alone for a couple hours sometimes. It's not a big deal."

That didn't sit right with me. Sure, she was responsible, but she was still a kid. A kid who was alone in an apartment complex where I didn't know all the neighbors or what kind of people lurked around.

I ran a hand over my jaw, debating. "When's your mom getting home?"

She shrugged, already pulling open the fridge and grabbing a juice box. "I dunno. She just said she'd be late."

Late. That could mean an hour. It could mean three.

I exhaled, leaning against the counter. "Tell you what, I'll stick around until she gets back."

Sophia's face lit up like I'd just offered her front-row seats to a Taylor Swift concert. "Really? Awesome!"

I checked the time on my phone. Nearly five. Samantha hadn't given me an exact ETA, but I figured she'd be home soon. And as much as Sophia seemed happy lounging on the couch, my firefighter instincts told me she probably needed more than a juice box for dinner.

I pushed off from the counter, stretching my arms. "Well, how about we get dinner started? That way, when she gets home, dinner will be waiting for her."

Sophia grinned. "You cook?"

I smirked. "I can handle the basics. Let's see what we've got."

We headed into the kitchen, and I opened the fridge, scanning the shelves. Some ground beef already thawed was a good start. My eyes drifted to the pantry—taco shells. Perfect.

"Tacos it is," I announced, pulling out the ingredients and setting them on the counter.

"Yes!" Sophia fist-pumped. "Mom makes tacos all the time. But she always says it's more fun when we cook together."

Something about that made my chest tighten, like I was stepping into a space I had no real claim to. But Sophia was already grabbing a pan, her enthusiasm contagious, and I couldn't bring myself to take a step back.

"Alright, chef," I said, ruffling her hair. "You handle the toppings, and I'll cook the meat. Deal?"

"Deal," she said, pulling out a cutting board.

As I browned the beef, Sophia chopped the lettuce with a little too much confidence for my liking, her tongue poking out in concentration. I stayed close, ready to step in if necessary, but she managed just fine.

"Mom's gonna be so surprised," she said, grinning.

I glanced at her, the warmth in her eyes making something settle deep in my chest.

"Yeah," I murmured. "I think she will be." I wasn't sure Sam would think it was a good surprise though.

The sound of a key in the lock made my stomach tighten. Sophia, completely oblivious to my hesitation, bounced on her heels.

"Mom's home!" she announced, grinning as the door swung open.

Samantha stepped inside, looking exhausted but instantly alert when she saw me standing in her kitchen. Her eyes flicked between me and Sophia, then to the counter full of taco fixings.

"You made it," I said, watching her reaction carefully.

She dropped her bag by the door and toed off her shoes. "And you're… making dinner?" Her gaze narrowed slightly, like she couldn't decide whether to be impressed or annoyed.

I cleared my throat, wiping my hands on a dish towel. "Figured we'd get a head start. Didn't seem right leaving Sophia to fend for herself."

Sam exhaled, tension still clinging to her shoulders. "I was only running a little late."

"I know." I held up my hands in surrender. "Just seemed like a good way to help."

Sophia rushed over, grabbing her mom's hand. "It was Evan's idea! And we're having tacos!"

Sam's gaze softened at her daughter's excitement, but when she looked at me again, there was something guarded there.

"I appreciate it," she said finally, walking toward

the sink to wash her hands. "I just... wasn't expecting you to stay."

I wasn't sure if that was an invitation to leave, but before I could say anything, Sophia was dragging her to the counter, pointing out every detail of our handiwork.

"Can Dad stay for dinner, please, pretty please?"

My eyes widened, and I barely stopped myself from choking on air. Dad?

Sam froze. Her back was to me, but I saw the way her shoulders tensed, her hands gripping the edge of the counter like she needed something solid to hold onto.

Sophia, oblivious to the sudden shift in the air, rocked on her heels, looking between us with hopeful eyes.

I didn't know what to say. My heart pounded in my chest, but I couldn't let it show. Couldn't let Sophia see just how much those words had cracked something open inside me.

Sam turned around slowly, her expression carefully neutral, but I caught the flicker of panic in her eyes before she smoothed it away.

"Your dad would love to stay," I offered hesitantly, "but I actually should be going. I'm supposed to meet up with some of the guys from church for a Bible study tonight."

Sophia frowned, crossing her arms. "I don't want you to go."

The words hit me square in the chest, far heavier than a seventh grader's plea should've been. I glanced at Sam, half-expecting her to step in, to tell Sophia not to put me on the spot like that. But she didn't. She just stood there, her expression unreadable, waiting. Maybe testing me.

I cleared my throat, rubbing the back of my neck. "Soph, I—"

"You made tacos," she interrupted, her voice taking on that stubborn edge I'd already started to recognize. "And we're all here. You can go to Bible study next time."

I chuckled, shaking my head. "That's not how commitments work, kiddo."

"But you're committed to us, too," she countered.

I didn't know what to say to that. Not when she was right.

Samantha finally spoke up. "Soph, that's not fair to Evan. He did us a big favor tonight by picking you up. But we can't ask him to give up his whole evening on short notice."

Sophia's face fell, her lower lip jutting out just slightly. "I know," she mumbled, poking at a stray shred of cheese on the counter. "I just... I like when he's here."

My chest tightened. I wasn't sure I had the right to feel the warmth that spread through me at her words, but I did.

"I like it when I'm here, too," I admitted.

Sam let out a slow breath, rubbing the back of her neck. She looked exhausted, the weight of the day pressing down on her shoulders. For a moment, I thought she was going to shut this whole thing down, send me on my way with a polite nod and a grateful smile. But instead, she met my eyes, something unreadable flickering across her face before she sighed.

"Stay," she said, pleading. "Just for dinner?"

I hesitated, but then Sophia brightened again, grabbing plates and setting them on the table like my staying was a foregone conclusion.

"Okay," I said finally, unable to fight the pull of this little family that wasn't quite mine but felt dangerously close to becoming so. "Just for dinner."

Sophia grabbed my hand. "Come on, I want you to try Mom's homemade salsa. It's the best."

I let myself be pulled along, but my eyes stayed on Sam.

She didn't look away.

After dinner, Sophia stretched her arms overhead and yawned dramatically. "Ugh, I have so much homework." My gaze followed her arms as she absently touched a necklace at her throat.

My chest tightened. "What do you have there?" I gestured toward her fingers, my voice coming out rough.

Sophia lifted the charm. "Oh, just my necklace. It was my mom's, but she said I could have it."

The silver heart caught the light, and for a moment, I couldn't breathe.

"It's very pretty," I said, my voice low, unsteady. My eyes locked onto Samantha's, and the past crashed into me.

I held the necklace out to her as we shared a blanket on the beach. "This is for you. It's not much, but it's a promise. I'll get you a ring when we get back to Chicago."

She had kept it.

Sam cleared her throat, breaking our eye contact. "Time for that homework, right?"

Sophia groaned but grabbed her plate and carried it to the sink. "Fine," she relented, dragging her feet toward her backpack. "But if I need help, I'm asking Evan." She shot me a pointed look, daring me to refuse.

I smirked. "I'll be right here."

Satisfied, she trudged down the hall to her room, leaving me alone with Sam in the quiet of the apartment.

She turned to the sink, rinsing off a plate, and I took the towel beside her without a word. We worked in silence for a few minutes.

But I felt her.

Felt the warmth of her body just inches from mine. Caught the way she tucked her hair behind her ear, exposing the graceful curve of her neck. Noticed the tension in her shoulders, like she was bracing for something.

I was bracing too. I stepped behind her, caging her with my arms on either side.

"You kept it," I said quietly.

"For her," she insisted, her breath shaky.

"I don't believe you," I replied in a whisper, my lips just centimeters away from her neck.

She shivered but didn't try to move away. I could hear her breathing, feel the heat radiating off her skin. My fingers curled against the surface beside her, itching to touch her—to trace the delicate line of her throat, to remind her of everything we'd once been.

Her voice was barely above a whisper. "It doesn't

matter what you believe."

But it did. It mattered more than I wanted to admit.

I lowered my head slightly, close enough that I could catch the faint scent of her shampoo—something light and familiar, something that sent me spiraling straight back to spring break, to stolen kisses and whispered promises.

"Samantha." Her name was rough on my tongue, filled with everything I couldn't say.

She squeezed her eyes shut, shaking her head. "Don't."

With one more shaky inhale of her scent, I stepped away, recreating the distance between us.

The past few weeks had been a slow burn, a constant push and pull between us. Some days, it felt like we were slipping into something easy, natural. Other days, the walls between us shot back up, a stark reminder that too much had been left unsaid.

And then there were nights like this.

Nights where the air felt heavier, thick with something neither of us seemed ready to name.

I wanted to ask her.

I wanted to say something—anything—to get a read on what she was thinking. Did she feel the same pull I did? Did she notice the way we kept orbiting each other, caught in some gravitational force we couldn't seem to escape?

But I didn't.

Instead, I cleared my throat and reached for the next dish. "You really do make a mean salsa."

Sam seemed grateful for the offering of a distraction. "Is that your way of saying you want to take some leftovers home?"

"Maybe," I admitted, my grin easy, despite the tension in my chest.

She shook her head, drying her hands. "I can pack some up for you."

I watched her move, tucking away leftovers, and it hit me—this was what home looked like. Not the Mercer estate with its cavernous rooms and cold perfection. Not the bachelor apartment I'd barely made my own.

This.

This simple, quiet moment in a tiny kitchen with dishes in the sink and a woman I couldn't stop thinking about. I wanted to step up behind her again and wrap my arms around her waist. I wanted to run my nose along the long line of her neck and feel her relax into my embrace.

I exhaled, forcing myself to look away.

I wasn't here to stir things up, not when Sam was

still figuring out how to let me in. Not when Sophia was the important thing. Not when I was still the guy who'd abandoned her after a quick romp that left her a single mother.

Not when I was still figuring out if I had the right to hope for more.

Sam turned, brushing a loose strand of hair behind her ear. "Sophia should probably say good night before you go."

I nodded, grateful for the excuse to see my daughter once more before leaving. "I'll go find her."

I found Sophia at the small desk in her room, her head propped on one hand as she stared at her math worksheet like it had personally offended her.

"Giving you trouble?" I asked, leaning against the doorframe.

She looked up and sighed. "It's boring."

I chuckled. "I can't argue with that. But you're smart—you'll knock it out in no time."

She straightened a little at the compliment, then frowned. "Are you leaving?"

I stepped inside, ruffling her hair. "Yeah, kiddo. It's getting late."

Her expression dimmed, but she nodded. "Okay... Can I walk you out?"

I hesitated, glancing toward the kitchen where

Sam was tidying up. "You sure? It's dark out."

She rolled her eyes. "I'm not scared of the dark."

"Of course not," I said, amused.

She grabbed a hoodie off the back of her chair and slipped it on before bounding past me into the hallway. "Mom, I'm walking Dad out!"

"Don't take too long," Sam called back.

Sophia grabbed my hand and tugged me toward the door. "Come on."

We stepped outside, the night air cool and still.

Sophia swung our joined hands between us. "Are you coming over tomorrow?"

I glanced down at her, my chest tightening. "I don't know. Would you want me to?"

She gave me an exasperated look. "Obviously."

I swallowed, nodding. "Then I'll try."

She turned to me suddenly, her brown eyes wide and searching. "Why aren't you and Mom together?" The question hung between us, innocent and heavy all at once.

I paused, the words stalling in my throat as I searched for the right way to explain the complexities of adult relationships to a young heart. The crickets chirped their nightly serenade, providing a gentle soundtrack to my internal struggle.

"Life's... complicated, Soph," I began slowly,

choosing each word with care. "Sometimes people need different things, or they change, and it doesn't mean they don't care about each other, or about you."

Sophia pondered that, her brows furrowing as she considered my words. "But you're still friends, right?"

"Absolutely," I assured her, my heart swelling at her hopeful expression. "And no matter what happens between your mom and me, I'm always going to be here for you. That's a promise."

Her smile was all the reward I needed, and she threw her arms around my neck in a hug that squeezed the breath from my lungs. The simple joy of her embrace grounded me, solidifying my commitment to her and the complicated dance of co-parenting with Samantha.

"Thanks, Dad," she whispered, and it was like music to my ears.

"Anytime, baby girl." My words were barely audible, whispered into the dusk. I wanted to tell her everything, to pour out the torrent of feelings for her mother that I kept dammed up behind a carefully constructed wall. But fear held me back—the fear of reaching out only to have those feelings slip through my fingers like smoke. And the knowledge that Sophia couldn't be the one I shared those feelings with.

That answer seemed to satisfy her, because she gave my hand one last squeeze before letting go. "Good night."

"Good night, kiddo."

She waited until I was at my apartment door before giving a little wave and heading back inside. I stood there for a moment, watching until the door shut behind her.

Then, with a deep breath, I let myself in, shutting the door on the part of me that ached to turn back. I let out a deep sigh, allowing myself that moment to soak in the quiet calm of the evening. My thoughts drifted to Samantha—the way her eyes crinkled when she truly smiled, how she could communicate with Sophia without a single word. My chest ached with the longing to reconnect, to somehow mend what had frayed between us.

I had to have patience, though.

There was something freeing in acknowledging the slow pace of healing, of rebuilding trust. I knew it wasn't about grand gestures or sweeping declarations—it was the daily effort, the small moments that wove together to create something stronger. That was the kind of dad I was going to be.

CHAPTER 18

Samantha

The letter felt like a brick in my hands, the words "coverage denied" stamped across the top in an unforgiving bold font. My stomach twisted as I read through the paragraphs of sterile, impersonal language explaining why the insurance company had decided my daughter's quality of life wasn't worth the cost of an ICD.

My grip tightened, crinkling the edges of the paper as my pulse pounded in my ears. No. No, this couldn't be happening. Sophia needed that device. She deserved it. It wasn't optional. It was the only thing standing between her and the very real possibility that her heart could stop again just because she dared to do normal teenager activities, like run around in the sunshine.

I sucked in a breath, willing my hands to stop shaking. I didn't have time to break down. I needed to fix this. There had to be an appeal process. A loophole. Something.

I could ask Evan. The idea flitted across my mind, uninvited and unsettling. He had money, of course—the Mercers were practically their own economy—but pride tightened around my chest like a vise.

Reaching for my phone, I scrolled past missed calls and unread emails until I found the number for the patient advocate I'd been working with. My finger hovered over the call button just as the front door swung open.

"Mom?" Sophia's voice rang through the apartment, light and cheerful, completely unaware of the storm raging inside me.

I swallowed hard, forcing a smile as I turned to face her. Evan stood behind her, his broad frame filling the doorway. His eyes met mine, and instantly, his expression shifted—from casual to concerned.

I looked away too quickly. I knew if I let him hold my gaze, he'd see everything. The fear. The desperation. The helplessness I couldn't afford to feel.

"Hey, sweetie," I said, pushing the letter onto the counter, out of sight. "How was school?" Evan had started picking her up after school any day he wasn't on shift at the station. She loved every second of it.

"Good!" Sophia beamed, oblivious. "Lola helped me with my math again, and I think I actually get it now."

"That's great," I murmured, barely processing her words. "Can you grab your laundry for me?" I needed her distracted until I could get myself under control.

Evan didn't speak right away, but I felt him watching me. He wasn't the kind of man you could fool for long.

"Sam?" His voice was low, careful.

I busied myself grabbing a glass from the cabinet. "What?"

"You okay?"

"I'm fine," I said too quickly, too clipped. I could almost hear the way his jaw tightened at the obvious lie.

I turned to the sink, pretending to fill the glass, but in the next second, I felt the warmth of his presence just behind me.

"Talk to me," he said, quieter this time.

I hesitated, my fingers gripping the counter. He

was the last person I wanted to admit this to. Because if I said it out loud, it became real. And if he offered to fix it... I wasn't sure I could handle that, either.

I mustered every ounce of strength and spoke with a firmness I didn't feel. "I said it's nothing. I don't owe you every little detail about my life, Evan."

"This isn't about owing me anything. You're upset, and I—"

"You *what?*" I cut in, turning to face him fully. The frustration, the fear, the sheer weight of it all finally cracked through. "You swoop in when it's convenient? You get to decide when you care?" My voice wavered at the end, betraying me. I hadn't meant to let that slip out.

Evan flinched, just barely, but I saw it. A flicker of something—hurt, regret, maybe even guilt—before his expression steeled over. "That's not fair," he said, his voice low and controlled, but not cold.

I let out a short, humorless laugh. "Fair?" I shook my head. "You don't get to come in here, acting like you suddenly have a say in my life just because you're around now. I've done everything on my own for fourteen years. I don't need you."

A tense silence stretched between us.

"I'm not trying to take over your life," he said

finally, quieter now. "But I care about Sophia. And whether you want me to or not, I care about you."

I sucked in a breath, my heart stumbling over itself.

Evan exhaled sharply, raking a hand through his hair. "Look, I don't know what's going on, but you don't have to do everything alone, Sam." His voice softened, but his eyes never left mine. "You *don't*."

The fight drained out of me, leaving only exhaustion in its place. I pressed my fingers to my temple, willing the pressure in my head to ease. "It's time for you to go home, Evan."

Evan didn't move. He just stood there, his gaze locked onto mine, steady and unreadable. "Sam—"

"I mean it." My voice was quieter now, but no less firm. "Go home."

A muscle ticked in his jaw. For a second, I thought he might argue, might push back the way he always did. But then he exhaled sharply, nodded once, and stepped back. "Alright."

He moved toward the door, but before he reached it, he paused, glancing over his shoulder. "This isn't over."

Something in my chest tightened. "Evan—"

"I don't give up that easy," he said, his voice firmer this time. And then, without waiting for a response, he walked out. But not without saying a quick goodbye to Sophia before he did.

The door clicked shut behind him, leaving behind an absence I felt far too deeply. I exhaled, pressing my fingers against my temples. I couldn't let him bulldoze his way into my life, into my problems.

But Evan Mercer had never been the type to back down.

And, apparently, neither was I.

The next afternoon, I shrugged into my coat behind the library desk. Just a few more minutes before I could leave. I hadn't even noticed Evan approaching until his stack of books hit the counter with a dull thud.

I startled, looking up to find him standing there, his expression somewhere between confident and unsure—like he hadn't quite decided which way to play this yet. "Hey," he said, rubbing the back of his neck. "Didn't think you'd still be here."

"Just wrapping up. Sophia went to Kelly's house after school." I glanced down at the books he'd set down, my fingers tightening slightly on my purse strap. *The Single Dad's Survival Guide. Understanding Your Preteen. Connecting with Your Child After Lost Time.*

A lump formed in my throat before I could stop it. He wasn't just saying he wanted to be involved— he was *trying*. Studying, even. And for a man like Evan Mercer, who probably made every decision on instinct, that meant something.

I swallowed, forcing my voice into something light. "Light reading?"

He exhaled, rubbing the back of his neck, looking almost… sheepish. Evan Mercer, sheepish. That was new. "Yeah, well… figured I should at least try to get it right."

Something in me cracked at the quiet vulnerability in his tone. This was the same man who had stood in my kitchen last night, pushing and prying, frustrating me to no end. And yet, here he was, not demanding but *learning*. And it undid me just a little.

I could have made a joke. Could have brushed it off. Instead, I just swallowed and reached for the first book, scanning it and sliding it back to him. "It's a really good start."

His eyes flicked to mine, something quiet in them. "Yeah?"

"Yeah," I replied with a thready voice.

The tension stretched between us, heavy but not quite uncomfortable.

"I'm really sorry about last night," he said. "You

were right. You don't owe me anything when it comes to your private life. I just... I want you to know that I'm here for you. Both of you."

The sincerity in his voice cracked something in me, just a little. I traced the edge of the counter with my fingertips, avoiding his gaze even as my heart pounded in my chest. *Both of you.* It shouldn't have made my throat tighten the way it did, shouldn't have sent a warmth curling through me that I wasn't ready to acknowledge.

I swallowed hard and nodded. "Okay." It was all I could manage. Not quite acceptance, not quite rejection—just a small step toward something I still didn't know how to define.

I finished checking out his books and pushed them toward him. "Here you go. You heading out?"

He nodded. "Yeah. I'll walk you to your car."

It wasn't a question.

I hesitated, my instinct to say I didn't need him to. But that wasn't the point, was it? He *wanted* to.

So, instead, I just nodded, pulling my bag over my shoulder and heading toward the door, Evan falling into step beside me.

And for the first time in weeks, we weren't arguing. Weren't throwing up walls between us.

We were just... walking. Together.

"Would you tell me about Sophia when she was little?" he said suddenly, his voice carrying a warmth that melted into the surrounding silence.

The question caught me off guard, my steps faltering just slightly on the pavement outside the library.

I glanced up at him, searching his face. His expression was open—hopeful, even—but there was a hesitation in his eyes, like he wasn't sure if he was allowed to ask.

Would I tell him about Sophia when she was little?

The weight of the question settled somewhere deep in my chest.

For so long, her childhood had belonged to just *me*. Every late-night feeding, every scraped knee, every first word, every giggle-filled game of hide-and-seek. I'd memorized those moments, stored them away like treasures. And now... he was asking for them.

My first instinct was to keep them close. To remind him that he hadn't been there, that he hadn't earned them. But hadn't I just told myself I wanted to let go of the anger?

I exhaled slowly, my breath turning to mist in the evening air.

"She hated naps," I said finally, my voice quiet with nostalgia. "Even as a baby. I used to drive her around the block just to get her to fall asleep."

Evan let out a soft chuckle, shaking his head. "Sounds about right."

I smiled, just a little. "She also loved music. I'd sing the same lullaby every night, and she'd hum along—before she could even talk."

His steps slowed. "What did you sing?"

Something in my chest tightened. "Cecelia and the Satellite," I admitted. The song had played nonstop on the radio the year we'd gone to Florida. I could still hear it playing from the tiny Bluetooth speaker on a beach towel.

I glanced over at him, at the way his grip had tightened slightly on the books in his hand. He looked... wistful. Like he was trying to piece together a past he hadn't been given.

"I sang her name in place of Cecelia," I explained. The lyrics drifted through my mind and I hummed a few bars.

For all the things my eyes have seen
The best by far is you.

I froze when Evan's voice crackled to life and he softly sang the last lines of the chorus. "I'd keep you safe, I'd keep you dry. Don't be afraid, Sophia, I'm the satellite. And you're the sky."

And for the first time, I let myself feel it—not just the resentment, but the ache. The sadness that he *hadn't* been there. I swiped at my eyes, wishing I could prevent the tears from falling.

"She took her first steps holding onto the coffee table," I found myself saying. "Then let go and ran straight into my arms."

Evan swallowed hard.

For a few steps, neither of us spoke. The air between us felt different—as if we'd stepped into uncharted territory and neither of us quite knew what to do with it.

"Did she ever go through a tomboy phase?" Evan asked, pulling me out of my reverie.

"Sort of," I answered, trying to steady my voice. "She was definitely more into climbing trees than playing with dolls. Always giving me mini heart attacks."

"She takes after her mom. Strong and determined."

The compliment caught me off guard, and for a split second, I wondered if his words were meant for me or just another extension of his affection for Sophia. It was a tightrope walk inside my mind, balancing between the desire to lean into this new dynamic with Evan and the instinct to keep him at arm's length. Was his growing attachment a sign of something more, or was I simply the gatekeeper to his daughter's world?

"Thank you, Evan," I said, my voice shaky with emotion. "But honestly, I think she's a lot braver than I am."

"Bravery comes in many forms, Samantha," he replied, his gaze never wavering. "And sometimes, it's a single mother doing whatever it takes for her child."

My breath caught in my throat at his words, resonating with a truth I often tried to ignore. Evan's unwavering attention told me he saw beyond the facade of the composed professional, into the depths of someone who fiercely loved her daughter but feared what opening up could mean. Could I let him in, allow those barriers to fall? Or would the act of trusting him prove to be my greatest vulnerability yet?

Then, finally, he cleared his throat. "Thanks for telling me," he said, his voice quieter now.

I nodded, hugging my coat tighter around myself as we reached my car.

He stopped beside me, shifting his weight like he

wasn't quite ready to leave yet. "I know I missed a lot," he said. "I can't change that. But I want to be here now."

I hesitated, my fingers tightening on my keys.

I wanted to believe him. I really did. And yet, the doubt gnawed at the edges of my thoughts, sharp and insistent.

Of course he wanted to be here *now*. Now that he knew about Sophia. Now that he had a tangible reason to stay. But what if that was all it was? What if, without her, there would be no reason for him to stand outside my car, looking at me like I mattered?

I swallowed against the lump in my throat, my grip on my keys so tight the metal edges dug into my palm. "I know you do." My voice came out softer than I intended.

His gaze searched mine, something unreadable flickering across his face. "That's gotta count for something, right?"

I forced a smile, but it felt brittle. "It does." And maybe that was true. Maybe it counted for a lot. But it didn't change the fear curling in my stomach, the fear that if it weren't for Sophia, he wouldn't be standing here at all.

I took a small step back, needing space, needing air. "I should go."

For a second, he looked like he might say something else, might push a little further. But then he nodded. "Yeah. Drive safe."

I slid into my car, shutting the door between us before my resolve could waver. As I pulled away, I caught one last glimpse of him in my rearview mirror—hands on his hips, head tilted slightly, like he was still trying to figure me out.

I wished him luck. I wasn't sure I even knew the answer myself.

CHAPTER 19

Samantha

The crisp autumn air carried the scent of cinnamon, caramel, and the faint smokiness of roasted nuts as I shifted in my seat at the library's fundraising booth. Around me, the Minden Fall Festival was in full swing—children darted past in costumes, their laughter blending with the cheerful twang of a bluegrass band playing near the main stage. Leaves crunched underfoot as families meandered between vendor stalls, admiring handmade crafts and sampling seasonal treats.

I, however, couldn't quite enjoy the festivities. My gaze kept drifting toward the sparse donations in the collection box.

I sighed and forced a smile as an elderly woman approached, dropping a few crumpled bills into the slot. "Thank you, Mrs. Calloway. We appreciate your support."

The woman patted my hand with a warm smile. "You always do such a wonderful job at the library, dear. I hope you reach your goal."

I hoped so too. The children's area renovations weren't cheap, and while we'd made progress, we were still far from what we needed. And Mr. Henley hadn't let me forget it.

I glanced across the festival, spotting Evan near the fire department's display. He was talking to Chief Daniel Bergman, his broad shoulders relaxed, his strong hands gesturing as he spoke. Even in a casual sweater and jeans, he had a quiet command about him.

As if sensing my gaze, Evan turned. His eyes immediately swept over me, his brow furrowing slightly before he murmured something to Danny and strode in my direction.

"How's the fundraiser going?" he asked, resting a hand on the back of my chair.

I let out a breath. "Not great. We've had some donations, but nowhere near enough."

His lips pressed into a thoughtful line. "Want me to make a scene? Maybe start an impromptu auction? I think I could convince some of the guys at the department to bid on—"

"Evan," I interrupted, laughing despite my frustration.

He grinned but leaned in slightly, lowering his voice. "Seriously, Sam. If you need more funding, just tell me."

I stiffened, shaking my head. "No, I'm not taking money from you."

His jaw ticked, but he didn't argue. Instead, he exhaled and gave my shoulder a quick squeeze before stepping back. "Alright. But I'll be keeping an eye on this."

Before I could protest again, Sophia bounded up to the booth, her friend Lola in tow. "Mom, can I go to the haybale maze with Lola? Her parents are here."

I hesitated, but Evan nodded. "Go ahead, kiddo. Just check in before the bonfire, alright?"

Sophia grinned. "Thanks, Dad!"

The word still sent a jolt through me every time I heard it, but it had become as natural to her as breathing. I met Evan's eyes, and something warm passed between us.

"She's fast," Evan remarked, his voice threaded

with amusement as his gaze followed Sophia's retreating figure.

"Always is when there's fun to be had," I replied, chuckling. It was one of the rare moments I didn't mind letting her run off—it was hard to begrudge her joy, even if her condition often kept my protective instincts heightened.

Evan turned his full attention back to me, a warmth in his eyes that I hadn't quite expected. "Do you want to go after her? I don't mind hanging around while she enjoys herself."

"Oh, I can grab her if you'd rather not wait," I offered, though the idea of staying with Evan held its own appeal.

He shook his head, a faint smile playing at the corners of his mouth. "I've got nowhere to be, and truth be told, it'd be nice to have some time—just us. Are you about done here?" he asked.

I nodded. "Yeah, Tiffany is coming to take over at four."

Evan glanced at his watch. "Good. That means we've got time."

I raised a brow. "Time for what?"

A slow, knowing smile curved his lips, the kind that made my stomach flip. "You'll see."

Before I could press him for details, Tiffany arrived, breathless and bundled in a thick cardigan. "Sorry I'm late! The line at the caramel apple stand was ridiculous." She plopped her bag down behind the table and grinned. "Go enjoy the festival, Sam. You deserve it."

I hesitated for a second, then turned to Evan. "Alright, mystery man. Lead the way."

He took my hand, threading his fingers through mine like it was the most natural thing in the world, and together we walked through the festival.

The afternoon sun hung low in the sky, casting everything in golden light. The scent of fried dough and apple cider wrapped around us as we passed booths and games, the sound of laughter and distant music filling the crisp air. I couldn't remember the last time I'd simply *been* at the festival instead of working through it.

"You gonna tell me where we're going?" I asked as Evan steered me toward the quieter side of the fairgrounds.

"Patience, Sam," he teased.

I huffed, but a smile played at my lips.

A few minutes later, we stopped in front of the haybale maze. I frowned. "We already did this, remember?"

"Yeah," he said. "But last time, we had an audience."

Before I could respond, Sophia ran up to us, her friend Lola trailing behind. "Oh! Are you guys going in? Can I do it again?"

Evan chuckled. "I was actually hoping to get your mom lost in there for a bit."

I felt my cheeks grow warm at his flirtatious words. Sophia grinned, then nudged Lola. "Come on, let's go find something fun before the bonfire starts."

As the girls darted off, Evan turned to me. "Alone at last."

I folded my arms. "And this is where you wanted to take me? Into a maze where there's a decent chance I'll leave you behind if you take too long?"

He smirked. "Not a chance. You'd miss me too much."

I rolled my eyes, but warmth spread through my chest.

We stepped inside, the walls of golden straw closing us in, muffling the festival noise. A few turns in, Evan slowed, letting his fingers brush against mine before taking my hand again.

"So," he said lightly, "did you ever picture this?"

"What?"

"Us. Like this. Together at a small-town festival."

I swallowed, my heart thumping against my ribs. "Honestly? No. I used to think about it, in the beginning. What it would've been like if things had happened differently."

Evan's grip tightened slightly. "Me too."

A few more steps of silence stretched between us, the air thick with unsaid words.

Finally, he stopped walking. "Sam," he said, his voice softer now. "I know we can't change the past. But I want this. I want us."

The honesty in his voice sent a shiver through me.

"Evan..."

"I know you're scared," he continued, his thumb stroking the back of my hand. "I know trusting me isn't easy. But I'm here, and I'm not going anywhere."

I took a shaky breath. "What if we mess it up?"

His lips quirked. "Then we figure it out. Together."

The word settled deep inside me, cracking through the walls I'd built.

Together.

I searched his face, the sincerity, the devotion, and something in me caved.

I squeezed his hand. "Okay."

His breath hitched. "Yeah?"

I nodded, a small smile breaking through. "Yeah."

Evan let out a breathless chuckle, then, without warning, tugged me against him. His arms wrapped around me, holding me close, and for the first time in years, I let myself sink into it.

A half-hour later, we exited the maze and I found myself chatting with Krystal Storm near the cider booth. The FaithMark actress had her signature bright blonde hair tucked beneath a knit beanie. Her husband, Bryce, was talking to Evan about something at the fire station.

"I loved your last movie," I gushed. "It had everything—small-town charm, a snowed-in cabin, and a misunderstood cowboy who secretly writes poetry." I fanned my face as though overheated. "Sophia and I watch every single one together."

Krystal smiled graciously. "That's so fun. I love that you can watch them with her. But am I wrong, or are you making time for some real-life romance these days?" She glanced meaningfully toward Evan.

"What? Oh… No, we're just–"

She turned to him with a dramatic sigh. "Evan, help me out here. Doesn't Samantha seem like someone who needs a little romance in her life?"

Evan smirked, sliding his hands into his pockets.

"I don't know, Krystal. I think she's doing alright in the romance department."

My cheeks burned. Krystal raised a perfectly arched brow. "That's what I like to hear," she said with a knowing smile.

As she bounced off, I turned to Evan. "You didn't have to encourage her."

He grinned. "But it's fun watching you squirm."

I rolled my eyes, but the teasing warmth between us lingered.

We wandered for a while, stopping to admire booths and sample apple cider donuts. The ease between us was growing, but there was still an undercurrent of tension. This felt more like a date than anything we'd ever done together.

The thought sent a ripple of awareness through me. This wasn't just two parents spending time with their daughter at a festival. This was something more. And the way Evan kept stealing glances at me —the way his hand brushed against mine every few steps—told me he felt it, too.

We stopped at a booth selling handmade candles, the warm scents of cinnamon and vanilla curling through the crisp autumn air. I picked one up, inhaling deeply. "Smells like fall in a jar."

Evan leaned in, his shoulder brushing mine. "That the official librarian review?"

I laughed. "I'd say so."

I reached for my wallet, but before I could pull out any cash, Evan handed the vendor a bill.

"You didn't have to do that," I said, glancing up at him.

He shrugged. "I wanted to."

There was something in his voice, something steady and sure. It was such a simple gesture, but it made my heart twist. I was used to doing everything on my own—paying for every little thing, making every decision. But Evan kept stepping in, kept showing me, in these small but significant ways, that I didn't have to anymore.

I cleared my throat, willing my emotions to settle. "Well… thank you."

Evan smirked. "See? You can let me take care of you a little."

I shot him a look. "Don't push your luck."

But as I walked beside him, I couldn't fight the tiny smile tugging at my lips.

Because the truth was, it felt good—being seen, being cared for.

And maybe I was finally ready to let him take care of me. A little.

CHAPTER 20

Evan

The flames roared around me as I charged back into the burning apartment complex, the heat touching my skin even through my protective gear. Smoke billowed thick and acrid, stinging my eyes and lungs, even with the mask and SCBA I wore. But I couldn't stop. Not when there might still be people trapped inside, relying on me to save them. We'd cleared everything but the second floor, and the neighbors thought the old man in Unit 2D had been home.

"Eli, take the west corridor!" My voice didn't waver. It couldn't; too many were counting on me.

"Copy that, Evan," came the crackled response over the radio. I could hear the man's trust in my decision.

"Keep talking, and watch for structural damage," I reminded them, though they knew this dance as well as I did. We'd trained for moments like these, when the world narrowed down to flames and survival.

I moved methodically from room to room, my senses straining for any sign of life amidst the smoke-filled air. Sweat poured down my face, my breathing labored, echoing in my ears through the mask. Yet a strange calm settled over me, the kind that only comes when you're doing exactly what you were meant to do.

I opened the door to what I assumed was a bedroom. There, I finally spotted him, huddled by the closet, near the floor where the air would be cleanest.

"I've got him." I looked back toward the hallway and grimaced at the rapidly deteriorating conditions before shutting the door behind me. "I don't know if we can make it back. I need ex-fil from the Bravo side." We'd just have to go out the window.

I held out my hand to the man, just as a thunderous groan shook the structure. I whipped my head up to see the ceiling buckle, then give way with a deafening crack. Flaming debris rained down, headed straight for the man cowering against the wall.

I lunged forward, covering him with my body. Fiery chunks of wood and plaster struck my back, but I barely felt them. All that mattered was shielding this stranger with my own body, keeping him safe.

As the dust began to settle, I found myself somewhere else entirely. Somewhere I tried never to go. The scent of smoke gave way to the stench of stale beer and sweat. Pulsing lights and throbbing music filled my head. Screams of terror, not from this fire, but from one long ago.

I squeezed my eyes shut against the onslaught of memory, but it was too late. I was back in that nightclub, desperately searching for my little brother amidst the chaos. The sickening realization that I'd failed him, that I hadn't been there when he needed me most. The guilt, the grief, the searing pain that never fully healed.

"Mercer, status?" The chief's voice cut through the noise.

Tears burned my cheeks as I clung to the trapped man, my breath coming in ragged gasps. I knew I had to keep going, had to finish the job.

I choked out a response, forcing the last bit of air from my crushed lungs. "Trapped. Ceiling. Bedroom."

My vision blurred, and the world tilted sideways. I fought to stay conscious, to push through the pain and the memories. But it was a losing battle.

"Mercer! Mercer, you copy?" Someone was shouting my name, their voice barely reaching me.

The last thing I saw was my brother's face—not the man I was shielding, but Mason, caught in the haze of smoke and memory, his features blurred by soot and shadow, just like that night all those years ago. Even though I hadn't found him that night, this was how I always saw him.

In the end, it didn't matter how many times I faced down the beast or how many lives I saved. The one that mattered most was beyond my reach, a debt I could never repay.

Then the darkness took me, and I saw no more.

The sterile beep of machines pulled me back from the void, their rhythm steady and reassuring. I blinked against the harsh fluorescent lights of the hospital room, so different from the flickering dance of flames I last remembered.

I tried to speak, but it came out more as a moan. The air here was devoid of smoke, replaced by the antiseptic tang that clung to the back of my throat. My limbs felt heavy, leaden, reluctant to respond after being rag-dolled by falling timber and the fierce grip of unconsciousness.

A gentle squeeze on my hand drew my awareness. Blinking against the fluorescent glare, I turned my head and found Samantha standing by my side, her fingers entwined with mine.

"Hey," she murmured, her voice a soft caress against the sterile hum of the hospital room. Her eyes were red-rimmed, her professional composure frayed at the edges. Samantha always had this look about her—like she could handle anything—but right now there was a vulnerability there that I'd never seen before. Not even when Sophia had been in the hospital had she looked so out-of-control.

"Hey yourself," I replied, trying to muster a grin despite the dull ache in my chest. "You look beat." The attempt at humor felt hollow, but it was instinctive, like breathing or reaching out to shield someone from falling debris.

She sobbed a laugh. Or laughed a sob?

She shook her head, swiping her eyes as if she could erase the emotion from her face. "Well, you look like a ceiling fell on top of you."

"Is that what happened?" I took stock of my body, slowly becoming more aware of the throbbing ache in my shoulder, the sting of raw skin along my arm. "Huh. Guess that explains the headache."

Her lips pressed together like she wanted to scold me for making light of it, but something in her expression softened instead. "You could've died, Evan."

I knew that. Of course, I knew that. But hearing it in her voice—strained and barely above a whisper—made it feel heavier somehow.

"Yeah," I admitted. "But I didn't."

She let out a sharp breath, shaking her head. "You can't just—just brush that off like it's nothing."

I tilted my head slightly, taking her in—the way she stood rigid, as if bracing for something, the way her fingers clutched at the hem of her sweater. She wasn't just upset. She was scared. For me.

"Sam," I said gently. "I'm here. I'm okay."

Her eyes flicked up to mine, searching for something—reassurance, maybe. A promise neither of us could really make.

She exhaled slowly, arms wrapping around herself. "You scared me," she admitted again, quieter this time.

I wanted to reach for her. Wanted to pull her close and promise I'd always come back. But I couldn't do that. Because we both knew there were no guarantees.

So instead, I just said, "I'm not going anywhere."

And I meant it.

I wanted to say more, to bridge the gap between us with words, but sometimes words just weren't enough.

"Sometimes, I think God's been nudging me in directions I've been too stubborn to follow," she confessed, her voice barely above a whisper.

"You? Stubborn?"

A ghost of a smile traced her lips. "I know. Hard to believe."

She let out a soft breath, her fingers smoothing over the edge of my hospital blanket like she needed something to do with her hands. "But I'm serious. I spent so long being angry at you, Evan. At what happened. At what didn't happen. And now you're here, and I don't know what to do with that. It feels like God brought you here, but I don't know why."

I swallowed, my throat dry. "You don't have to know. We can figure it out."

She huffed a quiet laugh. "See, that's the thing. You say that like it's easy. Like all we have to do is try, and everything will fall into place." Her hands clenched into fists in her lap before she exhaled and forced them open again. "But I have a daughter to think about. And I don't get the luxury of hoping this works out. I have to know."

I let her words settle between us before whispering, "Will you ever forgive me?"

"Will you ever forgive yourself?"

Her question hit harder than I expected. Harder than anything her anger or silence had ever done.

I started to look away, but she didn't let me. Her eyes held mine, steady and unrelenting. There was no accusation in them now, just something deeper—something I wasn't sure I was ready to face.

"I don't know how," I admitted, my voice hoarse. "I've spent so long carrying this, I don't know who I am without it."

Her expression softened, and she squeezed my hand. "Then maybe it's time to put it down."

Put it down. As if it were that simple.

But wasn't that what I was supposed to do? Hadn't I spent years believing I had to atone for my mistakes, to be good enough, strong enough, selfless enough to make up for what happened? And yet, here I was, still weighed down by the same guilt, the same shame.

I closed my eyes, pressing my head back against the pillow. "I don't deserve that kind of grace."

She was quiet for a long moment before she whispered, "Neither do I. But that's the thing about grace, Evan. It's never been about what we deserve."

The words settled into my chest, sinking deep like rain into dry earth.

I thought about all the times I had tried to fix things on my own. All the years I had spent believing I had to carry this burden, to make up for what I'd done. And yet, no matter how hard I worked, no matter how much I punished myself, the guilt never left.

Because I wasn't meant to carry it alone.

I opened my eyes and looked at her again. Really looked at her. Sam, who had every reason to hate me, to push me away, and yet here she was, offering me something I didn't know how to accept.

A way forward.

"I don't know how to let it go," I admitted again, my voice barely more than a breath.

She gave me a sad, knowing smile. "You don't have to. You just have to let Him take it."

God.

The answer had been there all along, but I had spent so many years only peripherally approaching him, convinced it was all I could ask for. That I had to earn my way back. But maybe... maybe I didn't have to. Maybe I just had to surrender.

A lump formed in my throat, and for the first time in a long time, I wanted to pray. Not out of obligation, not because I was trying to make a deal with God, but because I couldn't do this anymore. I couldn't carry the guilt of my mistakes anymore. Not for sleeping with Sam, which God had obviously used for something as miraculous as the little girl who held my whole heart. I couldn't carry the weight of Mason's death anymore.

I took a shaky breath, my fingers still tangled with Sam's.

"I don't expect you to just trust me overnight," I admitted. "But I meant what I said, Sam. I'm not going anywhere. Not again."

She studied me for a long moment, her eyes searching mine like she was looking for cracks in my resolve.

"I lost everything that night. My brother. You. And I spent years trying to make peace with the fact that I didn't deserve to get any of it back. But you're right. It's time to let go of that guilt."

CHAPTER 21

Samantha

I sat in the sterile silence of Evan's hospital room, my fingertips tracing the cool, plastic edge of his bed rail long after his eyes drifted shut. The near miss played over in my mind like a broken record. What if the other firefighters hadn't been able to get to him? What if the fire had been too big?

I almost lost him. But he was here. Alive. That truth should have been enough to ease the tightness in my chest, but instead, a different kind of pressure built beneath my ribs.

The thought sent a fresh wave of panic through me. It wasn't just a fleeting fear—it was the kind that reached down into my bones and wrapped itself around my heart, refusing to let go. I'd spent years making decisions out of fear. Fear of losing Sophia. Fear of his family finding out and taking everything from me. Fear of Sophia's heart giving out.

Fear had kept me safe. Or so I thought.

But sitting here, watching the slow rise and fall of his chest, I saw the truth for what it was.

Fear was a liar.

Fear didn't make me strong. It had only built walls—walls that kept me from trusting, from hoping, from letting myself believe that love could be anything other than a risk too dangerous to take.

I had let it rule me for too long.

I glanced down at Evan's hand, still resting near his side, bruised but steady. This man—this stubborn, charming, honorable man—had come back into my life, and no matter how much I tried to push him away, he refused to let me. He wasn't just here for Sophia. He was here for me too.

And that terrified me.

Because if I let myself believe in this, in him, and it all fell apart again, I wasn't sure I'd survive it.

But as I sat there, the warmth of his presence anchoring me, another thought whispered through the fear.

What if it didn't fall apart?

Leaning back in the chair, I let my gaze wander over Evan's features—those strong lines gentled by sleep or pain, I couldn't tell. And as I watched him there, vulnerable yet so incredibly resilient, something within me shifted. It was as if the walls I'd meticulously built around my heart, brick by emotional brick, began to crumble.

I may have buried it under years of anger, resentment, and pain, convincing myself that it was easier to hate him than to admit how much I had missed him. But love had never really left. It had just been waiting—for me to stop running, for me to stop hiding behind my fears and finally face what my heart already knew.

I swallowed hard, my fingers tightening around the edge of his blanket. I needed to tell him.

It wasn't his heroics. And it definitely wasn't his last name. It was the gentleness in his touch, the patience in his voice when he worked with Sophia, even after the longest shifts. The way he stepped up when I needed a hand. It was the way he made me smile and the way he made Sophia stand taller. It was him.

I was poised on the edge of my seat, nerves humming like power lines in a storm. The words had formed a procession in my mind, ready to march out into the open. I glanced at Evan, his chest rising and falling with the steady rhythm that the machines around him dictated. My fingers twitched, yearning to intertwine with his, as I leaned forward.

"Evan," I began, my voice barely above a whisper. The air felt thick, heavy with unspoken confessions. "I need to tell you—"

The door burst open, and a boisterous group of firefighters poured into the small hospital room, their presence immediately filling the space with laughter and an unmistakable sense of brotherhood. They were a colorful blur of blue uniforms and bright smiles.

"Hey, look who's finally taking a break from saving kittens from trees!" Eli Woods joked, clapping the now alert Evan gently on the shoulder.

"More like getting beauty sleep, if you ask me," Matteo said in his Spanish accent, and the room erupted in chuckles, even from Evan, whose eyes sparkled with amusement.

"Guys, keep it down, will ya?" Evan's voice was warm, tinged with gratitude, as he greeted each one with a nod or a weak wave. "I'm trying to recover here."

"Come on, it's not like a roof fell on you or

anything," Jake said. The room groaned at his bad joke.

I watched them banter back and forth, sharing stories that only they could fully appreciate. They spoke of close calls, of times when they'd relied on each other implicitly, when trust wasn't just necessary—it was life-saving.

"I should let you all catch up," I said, standing up and smoothing out my skirt, feeling oddly like an intruder on this sacred reunion of sorts.

"Sam." Evan's voice halted me, and I turned to find his gaze soft but locked onto mine. "Thanks for coming."

"Of course," I replied, my heart skipping a beat at the intimacy of his thanks. "I'll bring Sophia by later, okay? She's been asking about her dad."

"Looking forward to it," he said, a genuine smile touching his lips. I loved the way he loved our girl.

"Take care, Evan," I whispered, smiling at the men who continued their vigil around him. With a final glance at the man who had quietly stolen my heart, I slipped out of the room and into the quiet corridor, leaving behind the warmth of friendship for the cool solitude of my own company.

Two days later, I balanced the pan of homemade lasagna in one arm as I turned the handle and pushed open the door to Evan's apartment. In my other hand, I clutched a bag holding a fresh loaf of garlic bread, still warm from the oven.

"Hey, it's me. I hope you're hungry," I called out, stepping into the familiar space that was beginning to feel like an extension of my own world.

From his spot on the couch, Evan looked up, his eyes lighting up with something that might have been relief or maybe just plain hunger. "You're a sight for sore eyes." His expression flashed with amusement. "And I'm not just talking to the food."

I chuckled, setting the food down on the kitchen counter. "I brought lasagna," I replied, though my stomach fluttered nervously at the thought of what I really came to deliver.

He watched as I moved around his kitchen with ease, putting everything into the fridge.

"Here, let me help," Evan said, starting to rise, but I waved him off.

"Stay put, you're supposed to be resting," I insisted.

He settled back, a small smile playing at the corner of his mouth, which did all sorts of things to my insides. It wasn't quite dinnertime, but I grabbed a cookie from the container I'd brought and wrapped it in a paper towel before delivering it to him on the couch.

"M&M," I said, handing it to him.

"Maybe I need to get trapped in a burning building more often," he said, taking it from my hand.

"Don't you dare, mister."

Evan chuckled lightly, but there was something in his eyes that hadn't been there before—a depth, a weight. I settled back into the chair beside him, my fingers tracing idle patterns on my jeans.

I swallowed hard, knowing it was time. No more running. No more hiding behind excuses or justifications. "There's something I need to tell you," I said.

"You can tell me anything," he said, his eyes dark and focused on mine.

"I'm scared," I admitted, my voice barely above a whisper.

Evan's smile faded. His jaw tightened, and his gaze locked onto mine, searching. He opened his mouth like he was going to say something, but then he closed it again, waiting.

I took a breath and forced myself to keep going. "I told myself that if I let you in, if I let myself love you again, history would repeat itself. And this time, it wouldn't just be me getting hurt. Sophia—" My voice broke. "She'd lose you, too."

Evan shifted slightly, wincing at the effort, but his hand found mine. His grip was warm, firm. "Sam," he said, his voice rough with emotion, "that won't happen. You never lost me. I've always been yours."

Tears blurred my vision, and I shook my head. "But I did lose you. That night, I made it outside and then you were gone. And I looked for you, Evan. When I got back to school, I desperately hoped you would call me." My voice caught in my throat. "I was so heartbroken. Then I found out about Sophia, I started looking for you. When I finally found out who you were, who your family was, I thought… if they knew about Sophia, they'd take her from me."

Evan's eyes darkened, and his fingers tightened around mine. "My family doesn't control me. They never have, no matter how much they tried. And they will never, ever take Sophia from you."

I let out a shuddering breath, nodding, but it wasn't just his family that had scared me. It was him. Us. What we could be.

"I believe you. I've always been yours," I whispered. "There's never been anyone else."

Evan stilled, his whole body freezing, as if my words had knocked the air from his lungs.

I didn't look away. I needed him to see that I meant it. That no matter how much time had passed, no matter how hard I had tried to guard my heart, it had always belonged to him. Impossible as it seemed, I had fallen for him fourteen years ago in a single week on the beach. And now, over six months, I'd only fallen deeper.

A muscle in his jaw ticked, and then, slowly, he exhaled. "Sam…"

I lifted his hand, pressing it between both of mine. "I'm not running anymore."

Something shifted in his expression, something raw and unguarded. He didn't answer with words. Instead, he reached for me, pulling me gently but firmly into his arms. I went willingly, sinking into him, my face buried against his chest. His heartbeat was strong beneath my ear, steady despite everything he had been through.

We weren't perfect. We weren't healed overnight.

But this?

This felt like the first real step toward forever.

He pulled back just enough to look at me, his fingers brushing a loose strand of hair behind my ear. His thumb lingered against my cheek, his touch reverent, as if he couldn't believe I was really here, really his to hold. I felt that last lingering doubt rear its head at me.

I swallowed hard, my breath shaky. "If you're only saying that because of Sophia... I don't want you to be stuck with me just because we have a daughter together. I'll never keep you from her."

His brows drew together, pain flickering in his eyes. "Sam, no. I love Sophia. But I also love you." His voice dropped to a whisper. "It's always been you."

My heart slammed against my ribs, the last of my defenses crumbling. I cupped his face between my hands, feeling the roughness of his stubble, the warmth of his skin.

And then he kissed me.

The moment our lips met, the world faded. There was no fear, no regret, no past mistakes looming between us. There was only Evan—the way he breathed me in, the way he held me like he'd been waiting a lifetime for this moment. His fingers threaded into my hair, pulling me closer, deepening the kiss until I forgot every reason I'd ever had to keep him at arm's length.

When we finally pulled apart, we were both breathless. His forehead rested against mine, his hands still cradling my face like I was something precious.

"I love you, Samantha," he murmured, his voice unshakable. "And I'm not going anywhere."

Tears slipped free, but this time, they weren't born of fear. They were born of hope.

"I love you too, Evan."

CHAPTER 22
Evan

The children's reading nook looked worse than I remembered.

I ran my hand along the edge of a low wooden table, its surface scarred with scratches and faint crayon marks that had been partially scrubbed away over the years. The air smelled faintly of old paper and lemon-scented cleaner, though nothing could disguise the mustiness clinging to the aging carpet beneath my feet. The shelves, once painted a cheerful yellow, were chipped and faded to a dull, lifeless beige. A couple of stuffed animals sat perched on top, their fur matted and their seams stretched thin from decades of tiny hands tugging them this way and that. It wasn't much to look at now, but I could see it—what it could be.

I muttered under my breath, crossing my arms as I took it all in. "Let's turn you into something worth remembering."

This wasn't just about sanding down furniture or slapping on a fresh coat of paint. This was for Sophia. For Samantha. For the life I wanted to build, one piece at a time. My chest tightened, but not in a bad way—not entirely. There was something else mixed in there, some spark of hope trying to claw its way past the doubt that always seemed to linger.

I pictured a little girl sitting cross-legged on a bright new rug, her face lighting up as she flipped through one of those oversized picture books kids love. Maybe other kids would sit beside her, giggling and sharing stories. And Samantha…she'd be there too. Not just watching, but smiling. Relaxed. Happy. That image—it stuck with me, made me stand a little taller. There was nothing I wouldn't do for her.

After my impromptu visit to the library, I went directly to Sam's apartment. She opened the door, and for a moment, I forgot why I was there. She wore a simple navy sweater and jeans, her hair pulled back in a loose ponytail, but there was something about the way she looked at me—her eyes full of happiness—that made me forget what words were supposed to sound like.

"Hey," she said, tilting her head slightly. "You're early."

"Yeah, well." I cleared my throat, stepping inside when she moved aside to let me in. The faint scent of lavender drifted in the air, mingling with something warm and homemade—Mexican food, maybe? "Figured I'd leave room for traffic. You know how packed Minden gets on a Tuesday night."

Her lips twitched, almost forming a smile, but not quite. "Sure. Traffic. Come on in."

The living room was neat and cozy, every corner carefully curated. A stack of library books sat on the coffee table next to a half-empty mug of tea. I shoved my hands into my jacket pockets, suddenly feeling too big and out of place in the small space.

"How's Sophia?" I asked before I could stop myself.

"She's good," Samantha replied, crossing her arms as she leaned against the arm of the couch. "She's still over at Kelly's house."

"Right." I nodded, pulling a folded photo from my pocket and holding it out to her. "I wanted to show you this. It's, uh, something I've been working on."

She hesitated before taking it, her fingers brushing mine briefly. I tried not to think too much about it as she unfolded the paper and scanned the three-dimensional rendering—a bright, colorful mural design, modular seating, shelves low enough for kids to reach easily.

"Wow," she murmured after a moment, her eyes still on the page. "What is all this?"

"Turns out the newly established Mercer Foundation has sponsored a renovation for Minden Public Library," I admitted, scratching the back of my neck. I'd been debating what to do with my trust fund ever since I had the blowup with my father. He couldn't take the money back, and I was determined to put it to good use. A charity was the obvious choice. "But I've got help lined up. The guys from the station are pitching in. I just—I wanted you to know how serious I am about this. About being there for Sophia. For you both."

She looked up then, her expression unreadable. I braced myself for skepticism, for questions, for anything that might poke holes in the fragile confidence I'd built up on the drive over. But instead, she surprised me.

"Why the library?" she asked.

"Because it matters," I said simply. "It's a place where kids feel safe, where they can dream a little bigger. And because...it's your place. I wanted to do something that connected us, something that showed—" I stopped myself, realizing I might've said too much.

"Showed what?" she pressed, her voice barely above a whisper.

"That I mean it," I said finally, meeting her gaze. "All of it. You, Sophia, Minden. I'm here. And I'm not going anywhere, Samantha. Not this time."

For a long moment, she didn't say anything. Just stood there, holding the printout like it might slip through her fingers. Then, slowly, she smiled.

"It's amazing," she said. Relief flooded my limbs, so strong I had to remind myself to stay steady. Samantha's approval mattered more than I'd let myself admit. I had worked on the library, not just as a way to prove I could be here for them, but as a tangible offering. Something real. Something solid. I wanted her to see that I wasn't just making promises—I was building something that would last.

She reached out, her fingers brushing over mine where I still cupped her cheek. For a moment, I thought she might pull away, but she didn't. She stayed.

"You're sure? There's still time to change anything you don't like," I said, brushing away the tear that was trailing down her cheek.

"It's perfect," she whispered, her voice softer, like maybe she couldn't quite believe it herself.

I swallowed hard, my thumb absently tracing a line along her jaw. "I meant what I said, Sam. I'm here. Not just for Sophia, but for you, too."

Her breath hitched, her lashes flickering as she searched my face, looking for any hesitation. Any sign that I didn't mean it. But there wasn't one. I'd never been more certain of anything in my life.

She let out a slow exhale, her fingers curling into the fabric of my shirt. "Evan…"

I didn't give her a chance to overthink it.

In one swift motion, I closed the distance between us, my lips capturing hers with a gentle yet insistent pressure. Her hands glided up my chest, fingertips tracing the contours of my muscles, and her body melted into mine, a silent affirmation of her answer.

I sensed the tension unravel within her, like a tightly wound spring finally being released, and my heart swelled with pride and deep satisfaction. Nothing felt as right as having her in my arms, where her warmth radiated and filled the space between us with an undeniable connection.

A few days later, I stood in the library with the contractor.

"Alright, so here's the vision," I said, tapping the rolled-up blueprint on the table. We stood in the children's reading nook, the faint smell of old books and dust hanging in the air. The morning sunlight streamed through the tall library windows, catching the floating motes stirred up by our movements.

"Think bright, think inviting," I continued, gesturing toward the faded carpet beneath our feet. "We're talking soft colors, maybe something like a pale blue or green that doesn't scream 'institutional,' you know? And definitely some beanbags or comfy chairs for the kids to flop onto. Maybe even one of those little play tents—Sophia loves those."

"Yeah, I can see it," the contractor, a stout guy named Dale with a pencil tucked behind one ear, nodded as he scribbled notes. His voice was gruff but not unkind. "You're looking at ripping out this old furniture first, though. Some of this is from, what, the seventies?"

"Sixties, maybe," I said, crouching down to give one of the wooden shelves a firm shake. It groaned under my hand, wobbly enough to make me wince. "Definitely not safe for kids. This has gotta go. All of it."

"Got it," Dale said, flipping his clipboard shut. "I'll get my guys in here next week to start on the flooring and paint after you clear this stuff out. And we'll get new shelving units from Todd Flynn, I think."

By the time we started clearing out the space, the sun had shifted higher in the sky, spilling golden light onto the patchy carpet. Samantha showed up first, her sleeves already pushed up as if she meant business. She didn't say much, just gave me a quick nod before heading straight for one of the ancient armchairs in the corner.

"Careful," I called over. "That thing might crumble to dust if you touch it wrong."

"Then we're doing this place a favor," she shot back, her tone dry but her lips twitching in what might've been the hint of a smile. Progress.

A few minutes later, two of the firefighters from the station, Jake and Bryce, arrived, hauling work gloves and a dolly between them. Jake clapped me on the shoulder. "So, this is what you're moonlighting as now? Furniture mover for hire?"

"Only for the right cause," I said, grabbing one end of a rickety bookshelf.

"Great," Jake said with a grin. "Because this is exactly how I wanted to spend my day off."

"Less talking, more lifting," Bryce cut in, already stacking a pile of warped picture books into a box.

He glanced at Samantha, who was tugging at the stubborn armchair. "You need a hand with that?"

"Not yet," Samantha replied, grunting as she gave the chair a sharp tug. It scraped across the floor with an earsplitting squeal, and she looked up triumphantly. "There."

As we worked, the room began to take on a different energy. The cluttered, dusty space slowly opened up. My muscles burned as I hauled out decades-old furniture, but I didn't mind. Each piece I carried felt like shedding another layer of doubt, clearing the path to something better.

The scrape of the old bookshelf against the worn wooden floor echoed in the nearly empty room. I leaned into it, pushing with my shoulder until it slid into place near the growing pile by the wall. Sam said she already had someone coming to pick up the old shelves later today. My gloves were covered in a fine layer of dust, and I could feel the sting of sweat trickling at the back of my neck despite the cool air inside the library.

"Hey, Evan," Samantha said after a while, her voice cutting through the sound of Jake dragging an empty shelf toward the door. She was standing near the window, a faint sheen of sweat on her brow.

"Can you grab these boxes? I want to set up a small temporary kids section by the front desk."

"Of course." I moved to her side and turned to survey the space from her perspective.

For a moment, we stood there, side by side, looking at the half-cleared room. It wasn't much yet, but for the first time, I could really see it—the bright colors, the cozy corners, the laughter of kids filling the space.

"Alright, break's over!" Jake called, clapping his hands together. "Let's get this done before Bryce starts charging us overtime."

"Back to work," I said, grinning as I grabbed the box. Every lift, every step, every bead of sweat—it was all worth it. Because this wasn't just about renovating a library. It was about building something real.

Before I got too far, Samantha stepped close, lifting onto her tiptoes to press a kiss to my cheek. "Thank you," she said with a soft smile. "I still can't believe I agreed to let you do all this. But I'm glad I did."

The zing of energy from the contact kept me motivated all morning.

CHAPTER 23

Samantha

"This is ridiculous." I huffed, allowing Evan to guide me forward despite the blindfold covering my eyes.

"Just a little farther," he promised, his voice laced with excitement.

I shook my head with a half-laugh. "Evan, if I trip and break something, you're paying for the medical bills."

"Noted," he said, the grin in his voice unmistakable. "Just trust me."

Trust. That word carried more weight than it used to. I gave Sophia's hand a reassuring squeeze as she giggled beside me.

"This is weird," she said, her excitement barely

contained. "I feel like I'm about to be led to my doom."

Evan chuckled. "You're about to be led to something amazing, actually. Just a few more steps."

I let him guide me, his large hands steady against my shoulders. The scent of fresh paint and newly sanded wood filled the air, mingling with the familiar smell of books. We were in the library, I was sure of it, but whatever he had planned was beyond me.

I sighed, squeezing the small hand that clutched mine. "I don't mind surprises, I just prefer to see where I'm going. And it's not like I haven't seen most of the renovation. I do work here, you know."

Evan chuckled, his warm hand resting against my lower back. "Trust me, Sam. You're going to love this."

I exhaled slowly, trying to let go of my unease. Over the past few months, I had learned to trust him again. To let him into our lives in ways I never thought possible. And still, there were moments when the past whispered in my ear, reminding me of all the reasons I had built my walls so high.

But this was Evan. And he had never let me fall before.

"Okay, okay," he said finally. "Stop right here."

Sophia bounced excitedly next to me, tugging at my arm. "Can I take it off now?"

Evan's laughter rumbled behind me. "Go for it, kiddo."

I barely had time to process before Sophia's hands tugged the blindfold from my face, and I blinked against the sudden flood of light. When my vision cleared, I sucked in a sharp breath.

The children's area of the library had been completely transformed. The old, scuffed-up bookshelves had been replaced with new ones in dark wood, each lined with colorful, inviting books. A reading nook sat in the far corner, filled with oversized bean bags and a plush rug patterned with stars. The worn-out play tables had been replaced with sturdy wooden ones, complete with craft supplies neatly arranged in small bins. But the most breathtaking feature was the mural stretching across the entire back wall—a depiction of a whimsical storybook landscape, where rolling hills met a sky filled with floating lanterns, and a castle stood tall in the distance. I definitely hadn't seen that.

I pressed a hand to my mouth. "Evan...you did this?"

He rubbed the back of his neck, suddenly looking

sheepish. "Had some help. But yeah. What do you think?"

I turned in a slow circle, my chest tightening with emotion. "It's beautiful."

"It's perfect," Sophia added, already racing toward the bean bags. She threw herself onto one and grinned. "Mom, I'm never leaving this spot."

Evan's gaze never left me, as if he were waiting for something. For permission. For acceptance.

I stepped closer, pressing my palm against his chest. "Thank you."

His arm wrapped around my waist, pulling me into his warmth. "It's for the kids, but... I guess a little bit for you too." His voice softened. "You deserve everything good, Sam."

Tears burned at the back of my eyes, but before I could say anything, he cleared his throat. "And speaking of deserving good things... we need to talk."

I tensed at his shift in tone, pulling back just enough to meet his gaze. "About what?"

Evan's jaw tightened. "Sophia's ICD."

I immediately turned toward my daughter, who was flipping through a book as if she wasn't eavesdropping. "Sophia Rose—"

"I didn't tell him on purpose!" she rushed to say,

lifting her hands in surrender. "It just kinda... came out."

Evan crossed his arms, leveling me with a look. "Sam, why didn't you tell me she needed it?"

I turned back to him, guilt gnawing at my insides. "Because it's expensive. Because we've made it this long without one. Because she's careful, and I've done everything to make sure she's safe. I'll find a way to pay for it."

Evan exhaled heavily, his hands finding my shoulders. "You shouldn't have to do it alone." His voice was gentle, but there was steel beneath it. "And you don't have to."

I swallowed hard, fighting the overwhelming urge to push back. To stand my ground. I had spent so many years relying on myself because I had no other choice. But now, I did. And I didn't know how to let go.

"It's not your responsibility," I whispered, though my voice wavered.

His hands tightened ever so slightly around mine, grounding me, steadying me. "Yes, it is. She's my daughter, Sam. And even if she weren't, I'd still want to do this. I need to do this. I want to take care of both of you."

Tears blurred my vision. A lump swelled in my

throat, thick with emotions I wasn't sure how to process. Relief. Overwhelming gratitude. Fear of depending on someone when I'd spent so long learning how to survive alone. I shook my head, trying to find the right words. "Evan, it's too much."

"It's not," he countered, his voice firm but filled with so much tenderness it almost undid me. "And even if it was, I wouldn't care."

Before I could argue, he reached into his pocket, pulled out a neatly folded piece of paper, and pressed it gently into my palm. His fingers lingered, his warmth seeping into me like an unspoken vow. "It's already paid for."

I stared at him, then at the paper in my hands, my heart pounding. "What?"

"It's taken care of," he said simply, his voice steady, unwavering. "Turns out there is a program that covers medical costs for kids who need devices like this. No out-of-pocket expenses, no strings attached. She has an appointment scheduled for next week."

A disbelieving laugh escaped me—part relief, part exasperation, all love. My chest felt too tight, my heart too full. "You're serious? Some charitable organization just swooped in and paid for it?"

Evan nodded, his expression the perfect picture

of innocence. "Pretty amazing, right?"

Something in his voice made me narrow my eyes. I unfolded the paper, scanning the details until my gaze caught on a familiar name. Mercer Foundation —Sophia's Smiles Program.

I froze. My stomach dipped.

I lifted my gaze slowly, and Evan's lips twitched like he was really fighting a smile.

Oh. Oh.

"You—" My voice cut off as realization slammed into me. "Evan."

His grin finally broke through, sheepish but entirely unapologetic. "Technically, there is a charity organization."

I let out a breath, half a laugh, half something close to a choked sob. "You are the charity organization!"

He shrugged, his thumb brushing over my knuckles like that tiny bit of contact might soften the absolute audacity of what he'd just done. "I mean, technically... I may have started a charitable foundation since I needed to find a good way to use my trust fund, and I wanted to cover the renovation of the library for you. And I might have also specifically started a program for kids like Sophia once I found out what was going on."

"Evan Mercer."

"Okay, fine. I paid for hers myself," he admitted, his grin turning just a little cocky. "And I just named the program after our daughter. But in my defense, it is for kids like her. No parent should have to worry about how to pay for something that could save their child's life."

I stared at him, my heart a complete and utter mess. "You really did this?"

His expression softened, all teasing fading into something more real, more breathtaking. "Yeah, Sam. I did."

I glanced at Sophia, who was practically vibrating in her seat, her wide eyes darting between us like she couldn't decide if she was in trouble or about to witness the most romantic moment of her life.

I exhaled hard and shook my head. "You really shouldn't have."

Evan leaned in, brushing his lips against my forehead, lingering like he wanted to pour every unspoken promise into that one touch. When he pulled back, his voice was a hushed murmur, deep and certain. "But I did. What's the point of having resources if I can't take care of my girls?"

I inhaled sharply, the weight of his words settling deep inside me.

My girls.

It wasn't just about the money. It wasn't just about fixing a problem. It was the way he saw us—his instinct to provide, to love without hesitation or condition. It was the quiet, relentless way he showed up, proving over and over again that he was here to stay.

This was love. Not just spoken, not just promised—but proven.

My fingers curled around the paper, my throat too tight to speak for a long moment. But when I finally looked up, meeting his gaze, I saw nothing but quiet determination. Devotion. A man who had already decided that we were his future, and nothing—not even my stubbornness—was going to change that.

And in that moment, I let go.

"Thank you," I whispered, the words thick with emotion, meaning them more than I had ever meant anything in my life.

His arms tightened around me, pulling me close, and I let myself sink into the warmth and safety of him. For the first time in a long time, I felt like I wasn't carrying the weight alone.

I was his.

And he was mine.

And we were home.

CHAPTER 24

Evan

The hospital smelled like antiseptic and coffee —two things that didn't belong together but somehow always did in places like this. I'd parked myself at the nurses' station, leaning against the counter as I scanned the clipboard they'd handed me. The fluorescent lights above buzzed faintly, casting a pale glow over everything, but I forced myself to focus.

"Okay," I said, tapping the pen against the paper. "And you're absolutely sure she'll be under for the whole procedure? No surprises?"

"Mr. Mercer," the nurse—Tina, according to her name tag—said with a patient smile, "this is a very straightforward implant surgery. Dr. Patel is one of the best in the state. Sophia will be completely sedated, and we'll monitor her every second. You have nothing to worry about."

"Right," I said, nodding, though my chest still felt tight. "I'm just... you know. Making sure."

"Of course." Tina's smile was comforting, and she reached out to take the clipboard back. "She's in good hands. I promise."

"Good hands are great," I replied, shoving my own into my pockets. "Just make sure those hands are steady, too."

"Got it. Steady hands only," she said with a chuckle before disappearing down the hall. She was apparently very used to nervous parents questioning everything. Sophia had just been rolled off to surgery for her ICD implant, leaving us to wait anxiously. All my research and all the doctors had assured me that this was a very minor surgery with very low risk. But that didn't stop my heart rate from spiking as they wheeled my girl through the double doors.

I exhaled slowly, feeling the tension in my shoulders ease just a fraction. Turning, I saw Samantha sitting in one of the stiff plastic chairs by the waiting room window. Her arms were crossed loosely, but her foot tapped against the floor in a restless rhythm. She glanced up as I approached, her eyes meeting mine with an expression that was equal parts exhaustion and worry.

"You okay?" she asked, her voice quiet.

"They think I'm crazy," I said, dropping into the chair beside her. It creaked under my weight. "Am I overreacting?"

"Nope," she murmured, her gaze drifting back to the window. Outside, the sky had turned that washed-out gray that came before a storm. "She's strong, you know. She'll get through this."

"Yeah," I said, though my throat felt tight again. I wanted to believe it, needed to believe it. But the image of Sophia's small frame hooked up to monitors, her heart struggling against a condition none of us had seen coming—it stuck with me, refusing to let go.

When Samantha finally told me about insurance's refusal to pay for the implant for Sophia, I'd been furious at their incompetence and frustrated that she'd resisted telling me for so long. Then, I'd just been unimaginably grateful I had the means to provide what she needed. I'd also immediately set up a portion of funds from the Mercer Foundation so families could apply for the cost of these types of devices to be paid for by the non-profit. The program–I called it Sophia's Smile–was already being shared with hospitals around the country so they could direct families in need to the resources we had available.

We lapsed into silence for a while, the kind that wasn't uncomfortable but wasn't exactly easy, either. The hum of the vending machines filled the space between us, along with the occasional murmur of voices from other families in the waiting area.

Samantha shifted in her seat, uncrossing her arms. "Thank you," she said suddenly, her words so quiet I almost missed them.

"For what?" I asked, glancing at her.

"Being here. Doing all of this." She hesitated, brushing a strand of hair behind her ear. "You didn't have to."

"Yes, I did," I said simply, because there was no other answer. "She's my daughter, Sam. You have to know I'd do anything for her. For both of you," I amended.

She didn't respond, but something in her posture relaxed just a little. Her tapping foot stilled.

"I know I told you that I tried to find you. I didn't tell you that my father..." I paused, inhaling deeply through my nose. The sterile scent of antiseptic filled my lungs, and for a moment, it steadied me. "He's the one who interfered."

Her shoulders stiffened. I hated seeing that. Hated knowing my family had done this to her, to us. But I wasn't going to run from it now. Not anymore.

"I didn't know until I found you. But apparently he thought he was protecting his legacy or whatever garbage he tells himself to sleep at night." My voice sharpened, but I forced myself to soften it again. This wasn't about my father. This was about her. "But, Sam, I need you to know—" I leaned forward, elbows resting on my thighs, trying to catch her eye. "That'll never happen again. Never. I won't let it."

She finally looked at me, her expression unreadable. The fluorescent light above us flickered once, casting fleeting shadows across her face. I waited, letting the silence stretch between us, heavy but honest. If she needed space to process, I'd give it to her. After all, I owed her that—and so much more.

"How can you be sure?" she asked, her voice quiet but steady. There was no accusation in it, just curiosity laced with a cautious edge. "What if he tries? What's changed?"

"Everything," I said simply. "Me. I've changed."

Her brows drew together, creating a delicate crease between them. I wanted to reach out, smooth it away, but I kept my hands where they were. "I can't undo the past," I added, my voice dropping to a near whisper. "But I can promise you this: I'm here now. For you, for Sophia. No one—not my father, not anyone—is going to come between us again. Not unless I'm dead and buried."

The corner of her mouth twitched—just barely, but it was enough to send a ripple of relief through me. "That's a little dramatic," she murmured, finally meeting my gaze fully.

"Yeah, well, I've been told I have a flair for theatrics," I replied, cracking a small smile. It felt strange, unfamiliar, but good. Like sunlight breaking through clouds you'd forgotten could part.

Samantha exhaled slowly, her shoulders relaxing just a fraction. Her guarded expression loosened, though the walls she'd built so carefully over the years hadn't crumbled entirely. I didn't expect them to; I'd spent too long contributing to their construction. Still, there was a shift—a glimmer of something I hadn't dared hope for.

"Okay," she said after a long pause. Just one word, spoken softly, but it carried the weight of a thousand conversations we hadn't had and the possibility of the ones we still could.

"Okay?" I echoed, leaning back in my chair, giving her the space I knew she needed.

"Okay," she repeated, her tone firmer this time. A small nod accompanied the word, and though her lips didn't quite curve into a smile, there was a warmth in her eyes that hadn't been there before.

I stared up at the ceiling tiles. They were dotted with tiny holes, arranged in patterns that didn't quite make sense. My fingers found the small cross pendant hanging around my neck—something I hadn't worn in years until recently. Closing my eyes, I let the sounds of the hospital fade into the background.

I prayed for Sophia's safety during the surgery, trusting the Lord with a depth of peace I hadn't known in years. I didn't try to bargain or justify. I just let the prayer settle, releasing it into the unknown.

When I opened my eyes, Samantha was watching me. She didn't say anything, but there was something in her expression—a flicker of understanding, maybe—that made me feel less alone in that moment.

I paced so much the soles of my boots were probably wearing tracks into the linoleum. Every time I passed the window, I glanced out at the parking lot below, the endless rows of cars shimmering under the afternoon sun. It was a painfully ordinary scene, completely at odds with the storm twisting inside me.

Then the door opened and the doctor walked in —a middle-aged woman with kind eyes and a no-nonsense demeanor—it felt like the air got sucked out of the room for a moment, and I stopped mid-step, my pulse thundering loud enough to drown out everything else. Samantha stood from her chair across the room, her hand gripping the armrest as if it were the only thing keeping her steady.

"She's doing great," the doctor said, her voice even, calm. "The procedure went exactly as planned. The ICD is in place, and she's already waking up in recovery."

I didn't realize how tightly I'd been holding onto my breath until it came rushing out all at once. Relief hit me like a wave, nearly knocking me off balance. My knees wobbled, and I sat down hard in the nearest chair, dragging my hands over my face. "Thank God," I muttered, half to myself, half to the universe.

"Can we see her?" Samantha asked, her voice trembling just slightly.

"Not quite yet," the doctor replied gently. "Give us about thirty minutes, and someone will come get you."

"Thank you," Samantha said, her voice steadier now, though I could see the faint sheen of tears glistening in her eyes. She turned toward me, folding her arms across her chest. "You okay?"

"Yeah," I said, though my throat felt tight, like everything I'd been holding back wanted to spill out all at once. "Yeah, I'm good." I leaned forward, resting my elbows on my knees. "She's gonna be okay. That's all that matters."

The truth was, I wasn't sure how to describe what I was feeling. It wasn't just relief—it was something deeper, something that settled into the cracks I hadn't even realized were still there. For so long, I'd felt like I was running uphill, trying to prove I could be the kind of man they deserved—someone they could rely on, trust. And now, for the first time, it felt like I'd finally reached solid ground.

CHAPTER 25
Samantha

Sophia was released from the hospital the same day her implant was inserted, with instructions to keep an eye on the small incision and to take it easy. The first evening home, I was halfway through a chapter of my latest book, listening with one ear as she and Evan played cards at the kitchen table.

"Are you teaching our daughter how to play poker?" I admonished with a laugh.

Evan's eyes widened in mock innocence. "Of course not!"

I scowled at him. "She's only thirteen, Evan."

"We're playing Rummy, Mom," came Sophia's sassy reply.

I glared at Evan, catching the playful expression

there. He'd tricked me. I tossed a piece of popcorn at him. "Rude."

He chuckled, catching the piece effortlessly and popping it into his mouth. Sophia, grinning, leaned forward, resting her elbows on the table.

"So, Mom. I was thinking... One of the girls I know from school lived in those apartments that burned down." She glanced at Evan. "The one you were in, Dad."

My heart clenched at the memory of his hospitalization.

"Well, I know all those families lost all their stuff, right? So, I thought maybe we could put together a few things for them? You know, food, books, toys for the little kids or whatever?"

Her enthusiasm was contagious, and even before Evan and I exchanged glances, I knew we were on board. This was the heart of our daughter—always eager to help, always looking beyond herself. The girl had just had surgery herself, and here she was, wanting to help others.

"Let's do it," I agreed, matching her smile with one of my own.

Over the next few days, our kitchen became a command center, piles of supplies stacking up as we gathered items for the displaced families. Sophia made friendship bracelets for the girl from school, and I gathered toiletries and blankets. Evan reached out to a few firefighter buddies who donated extra clothes and household necessities.

"Mom, would you write the notes?" Sophia's request pulled me from my thoughts. "You have the neatest handwriting."

"Of course, sweetheart." My fingers lingered on the crisp paper, the pen poised as I thought of the words to convey comfort and hope.

We wrapped each package with care, and I couldn't help but marvel at the sweet nature of my child. She had faced her own fears, her own uncertainty, yet here she was, pouring out love to strangers.

The last of the tape sealed the final care package with a satisfying snap. I stepped back, admiring our handiwork. Evan's hand wrapped around mine, giving it a squeeze. Less than a year ago, I had assumed I would never see him again. Now, I couldn't imagine our life without him.

"Here, Soph. Let's pray over these and then we'll get them delivered." Evan reached his other hand out to her, bowing his head as he said a quick, heartfelt prayer of blessing and comfort over the families who'd lost their homes.

"Okay, let's get moving," he said, rolling up his sleeves and revealing those familiar, strong forearms developed from years of firefighting. It was hard not to watch him as he moved, each action deliberate and sure.

Sophia skipped ahead, leading us out to the parking lot where our old sedan waited. The trunk yawned open, hungry for the packages we carried. Evan took charge, arranging each box with Tetris-like precision.

A few hours later, after delivering the last care package to the extended-stay hotel in Greencastle where most of the families had been put up, we headed back to the car, tired but satisfied with a job well done. The evening air had turned crisp as the sun sank low. I pulled my cardigan tighter around me and glanced up at Evan, his silhouette painted against the dusky sky.

"She's a pretty amazing little girl," he began, his voice low and tender. "I want to do whatever it takes to make sure she's taken care of." He turned to face me, his kind eyes searching mine in the dimming light. "I know you might not be ready to take the next step with me... And that's fine. I'll wait as long as it takes. But I want to do whatever it takes to make sure she's legally my daughter. Her birth certificate or whatever."

I felt my breath catch, the simple sincerity in his words carving through the layers of defenses I'd built over time.

"Of course," I whispered, the lump in my throat making it hard to speak. He wanted to be her dad on paper. But he was already her dad in every way that counted.

His calloused hand reached for mine, rough from years of selfless service yet gentle as it enveloped my own. The touch sent a current of warmth spiraling through me, an affirmation of the connection that had weathered so much. "And whenever you're ready, Sam, I want to marry you."

My eyes widened in surprise. "What? I—What are you saying?"

"I love you," he said, a warm chuckle accompanying his words. "I'm ready whenever you are. Let's build something beautiful, not just for us, but for our little firecracker waiting in the car."

"Mom! Dad! Are you coming?" Sophia's voice rang out from the open window, filled with impatience and love all mingled into one.

Evan laughed, the sound rich and genuine.

"Coming, sweetheart!" I called back, squeezing

Evan's hand tighter.

And just like that, with the night wrapping around us like a promise, we walked forward together, ready for whatever lay ahead.

Slipping into the car, I couldn't help but bask in the lingering warmth of Evan's declaration, as if his words had settled over me like a comforting blanket. The dashboard clock glowed 8:07 PM, its light painting the interior with soft blue hues.

"What were you two talking about?" Her silhouette bobbed slightly as she leaned forward, mischief sparkling in her eyes.

I felt my cheeks redden. "Nothing, Soph."

"I thought you were going to tell her, Dad!" Sophia scolded. "Come on. You guys just need to get married already."

Evan laughed, reaching over to squeeze my hand where it rested on my lap. "Patience, kiddo. Some things take time."

Sophia huffed dramatically. "You've already waited forever. I mean, I'm practically a grown-up now. If you wait any longer, I'll be off to college before you two get your act together."

I turned in my seat, meeting Evan's gaze. He looked at me with that same unwavering steadiness he always had, the kind that made me feel safe, made me believe that maybe, just maybe, forever wasn't something to be afraid of.

"She's got a point," Evan murmured, his thumb brushing over my knuckles. "But no pressure. Whenever you're ready."

I swallowed past the lump in my throat, emotion thick in my chest. "You really mean it, don't you?"

"Yeah, Sam. I do." He reached into his pocket and pulled out a small velvet box, flipping it open to reveal a ring. My breath hitched, heart pounding. The diamond wasn't extravagant, but it was perfect —simple, elegant, timeless. Just like us.

"I've been carrying this around for weeks, waiting for the right moment," Evan admitted, voice thick with emotion. "I didn't want to push, didn't want to rush you. But I knew, Sam. I knew I wanted this—us—forever."

Tears welled in my eyes as I blinked rapidly, overwhelmed by the sheer depth of what he was offering. A lifetime. A home. A love that had never wavered, even when I'd been too afraid to reach for it.

Evan slipped the ring onto my finger, his hands warm and steady. "I love you, Sam. Always. Will you marry me?"

I cupped his face, pulling him in for a kiss—soft,

lingering, filled with every unspoken promise. When we finally pulled back, Sophia was practically vibrating with excitement.

Sophia groaned loudly from the backseat. "Okay, okay, enough kissing! Just say yes already!"

I laughed, shaking my head as I looked between them—the two people who meant everything to me. Fear had kept me from this for so long, but love? Love was stronger. Love had brought Evan back, had given Sophia the father she deserved, had given me the family I never thought I'd have.

I took a deep breath, feeling the weight of the moment settle over me in the best possible way. "Okay," I whispered, squeezing Evan's hand. "Yes. Let's do this."

"I totally get to plan the wedding," she demanded.

Evan chuckled, resting his forehead against mine. "Guess we better get started."

Sophia let out a shriek of excitement, bouncing in her seat. "Finally! This is the best day ever!"

Evan grinned, lifting my hand to his lips, pressing a kiss against my fingers. "Best day yet," he corrected. "There are a lot more to come."

And as we drove home—home, where we belonged—I knew he was right. Our story wasn't perfect, but it was ours. And it was just beginning.

Epilogue

The fellowship hall pulsed with warmth and laughter, the scent of pine, cinnamon, and something sugary filling the air. Strings of twinkling lights crisscrossed the ceiling, and the massive Christmas tree in the corner glowed with colorful bulbs, reflecting off the glossy tile floor. Kids darted between tables, weaving around clusters of firefighters and their families, their excited giggles rising above the hum of conversation.

I'd heard that the annual Christmas party was always a big deal, but this was my first. And I had to think it was better than ever.

Maybe because Samantha was by my side, her arm looped through mine as we moved through the crowd. We'd been married for a month, and I would never tire of introducing her to everyone I met as my wife. She looked lovely tonight, effortlessly beautiful in a deep-green sweater that brought out the warmth in her hazel eyes. The soft glow of Christmas lights reflected in her hair, and the scent of cinnamon and something distinctly *her* wrapped around me like a familiar embrace.

But it wasn't just how she looked—it was the way she carried herself. Graceful, but with that quiet strength I'd fallen in love with. The way she spoke to people, making each conversation feel important. The way she laughed, soft but rich, like she was savoring the moment. The way she squeezed my hand every now and then, as if to remind me she was there, that we were in this together.

I'd spent so many years believing I didn't deserve something like this. Like *her*. But God had given me a second chance, and I wasn't about to waste it.

Or maybe tonight was special because Sophia was nearby, shrieking with laughter as she and Nathan Wells's boys chased each other in a game of tag around the tree.

Or maybe it was the overwhelming sense of belonging pressing into my chest, the realization that this wasn't just a job, and these weren't just coworkers.

This was family.

True to my word, I hadn't spoken to my father since the last time I'd stepped foot in his office. My mother, on the other hand, had made the trip to Minden not once, but twice. Once to meet Sophia and again to attend her middle school choir concert earlier this month.

The meetings hadn't gone perfectly, but Samantha had encouraged me to let my mom try to earn a place in Sophia's life. I knew Sam's parents left even more to be desired than my own. I suspected she liked the idea that Sophia would have a grandmother who cared about her.

I felt Samantha glance up at me, her hand squeezing my arm briefly before we were intercepted by Bryce and Krystal. Krystal's cheeks were pink, her eyes shining with a secret she was clearly dying to spill. Bryce, on the other hand, had the kind of smug grin I recognized from months of working alongside him—like he'd just aced a difficult rescue and was waiting for applause.

"We've got news," Krystal announced, resting a hand on her stomach.

Bryce puffed up a little. "Baby Storm, coming this summer."

Samantha gasped, her whole face lighting up. "Oh, Krystal, that's wonderful!"

Krystal beamed as Bryce wrapped a protective arm around her. "Yeah, we're excited. And exhausted. And slightly terrified."

"Get used to that feeling," I said, smirking. "As far as I can tell, that feeling never really goes away."

A strange pang settled in my chest as I watched him cradle her growing baby bump.

I should have had that with Samantha.

I should have been there to feel Sophia kick for the first time, to bring home ridiculous midnight snack combinations, to hold Samantha's hand through every milestone. Instead, I'd missed all of it. And even though I knew there was no changing the past, I still felt the ache of everything we'd lost.

Samantha glanced up at me, something flickering across her face as if she could read my thoughts.

The conversation drifted, but as we moved on, Samantha didn't let go of my hand.

She was quiet for a long moment before speaking. "You're thinking about what you missed."

I sighed, rubbing a hand over my jaw. "Yeah."

She nodded, thoughtful. "I wish you had been there, too."

Her honesty sent a rush of emotion through me,

and before I could second-guess it, I turned to face her fully, brushing a stray curl behind her ear. "Maybe… we don't have to miss everything."

Her breath caught, her eyes locking onto mine. "What do you mean?"

I hesitated, choosing my words carefully. "I mean… maybe we could do it differently this time. Together."

Her lips parted slightly, surprise and something else—something softer—flickering across her face. "You're saying…?"

"I'm saying if you ever wanted to—if *we* ever wanted to…" I swallowed, feeling suddenly reckless. "I wouldn't mind starting over. Having that experience with you. From the beginning. Giving Sophia a little brother or sister?"

Her expression turned unreadable, and for a moment, I wondered if I'd overstepped.

Then, her fingers tightened around mine.

"I don't know what the future holds," she admitted, voice barely above a whisper. "But I do know that if I ever had another baby…" She paused, searching my face. "I'd want to do it with you."

A slow, deep warmth spread through my chest.

I grinned, pressing a lingering kiss to her forehead. "Good to know."

She let out a breathy laugh. "Don't get any ideas, Mercer."

"No promises," I murmured, reveling in the way she leaned into me.

And as we moved back into the party, the ache of the past eased just a little. Because the future?

That was still ours to write.

Sophia was still tangled up in the chaos of Nathan's boys, her laughter bright and uninhibited. Nathan himself stood by the dessert table with Rebecca, his arm slung over her shoulders.

"Still crazy about each other," I mused as we approached.

Nathan grinned as he caught sight of us. "Wouldn't have it any other way."

Rebecca rolled her eyes but smiled. "It helps that he still looks at me like I hung the moon."

Nathan squeezed her tighter. "That's because you did."

Samantha made a sound beside me, and when I looked down, her expression was unreadable.

But I felt her fingers tighten around mine.

I let the moment sit before teasing, "So, how's the bookstore gig treating you?"

Rebecca brightened. "It's amazing. Honestly, I think I've found my place."

Nathan nodded proudly. "She could sell anything. Half the people who walk into that store end up leaving with an armful of books they didn't know they needed."

Rebecca laughed, swatting his chest. "It's a Christian bookstore, Nathan. People come in to buy things."

"Not that many things," he shot back. "It's a talent."

Rebecca laughed before turning to Samantha. "And you? How's everything been with the library?"

Samantha's smile softened. "Good. The renovations for the children's section turned out even better than I hoped. And I get to watch kids fall in love with books every day."

Nathan grinned. "Sounds like a win."

Samantha nodded, her gaze flicking up to mine for the briefest moment before we moved on, weaving through the crowd.

I glanced down at her as we walked. "You really love it, don't you?"

She tilted her head, eyes dancing. "What, books? Of course."

"No." I stopped, brushing a thumb over the back of her hand. "This. The life you've built."

Her smile faltered for just a second, something

unspoken passing between us. Then she exhaled, a happy, contented sigh. "Yeah. I really do."

Something tightened in my chest, and before I could overthink it, I dipped my head, pressing a slow, lingering kiss to her temple.

Her breath hitched.

And for a moment, the party blurred around us— the laughter, the music, the bright twinkle of Christmas lights all fading into the background.

Then, a loud baby wail pierced the air, and Samantha huffed a quiet laugh as I pulled back, shaking my head. "Well, that was a moment."

"Welcome to life with a big family," she teased, nudging me forward. "Come on. Let's go see who's crying."

We found Jake and Monica nearby, their six-month-old daughter fussing in Monica's arms.

"She's getting so big," Samantha cooed, reaching out a finger for the baby to grab.

Jake, ever the quiet one, gave a weary nod. "Yeah. And louder."

Monica shot him a look. "She just... knows how to make herself heard."

Jake met my gaze with a smirk, and I chuckled. "Sounds familiar." Jake had a reputation for being the loudest member of the department.

Samantha and Monica continued talking, their voices dipping into quiet happy tones, while I glanced across the room.

Elijah and Carla stood near the fire truck bay doors, deep in conversation, until Elijah spotted us and waved us over. "Look who finally closed the deal," he said, gesturing between me and Samantha.

I shook my head. "Still can't believe she married you."

Elijah grinned. "Right? Best con job I ever pulled."

Carla rolled her eyes but leaned into his side. "Figured I'd keep him out of trouble."

"Good luck with that," I muttered, earning a round of chuckles.

Samantha nudged Carla's arm. "You guys seem really happy."

"We are," Carla said, her voice full of contentment.

I narrowed my eyes at Elijah. "You guys thinking about kids yet?"

Elijah shrugged, but his grin gave him away. "Let's just say we're not *not* thinking about it."

Carla laughed. "Translation: He's already picked out names."

I smirked. "Man's got a plan."

Elijah clapped me on the back. "You know me. Always prepared."

Samantha squeezed my hand again as we moved toward the center of the room, her expression softer than before.

I let my gaze sweep over the firehouse, over the people who had become my family.

This place. These people.

Somehow, despite everything I had lost, despite the years of regret and loneliness, God had given me more than I ever could have imagined.

Bryce and Krystal stood off to the side, lost in their own little world, his hand never straying far from her. I'd heard the story about how he'd been in love with her in high school. Their second chance had come more than a decade later, when Krystal returned to town. And now, God was blessing them with a child. A new beginning.

Jake and Monica sat near the Christmas tree, Monica rocking a sleepy baby in her arms while Jake leaned in, whispering something that made her smile. Jake had shared how Monica's car accident had given her amnesia and almost destroyed their relationship. Their love hadn't come without its struggles, but here they were, stronger than ever.

Parents. Partners. Proof that love could conquer anything.

Nathan and Rebecca moved through the crowd, greeting everyone with easy smiles. They were the steady ones, the couple that had been tested and had come through the fire more in love than before. It wasn't easy to see a marriage through fifteen years, but Nathan said every day was another chance to choose to love each other.

Elijah and Carla laughed together near the dessert table, their hands intertwined, completely at ease. Their relationship had ended what had been a decades-long feud between two of Minden's oldest families.

Everywhere I looked, I saw proof of His grace. Of His mercy.

Second chances.

Every single couple in this room had been given one. And somehow, against all odds, so had I.

I let my gaze sweep over the room once more. Every one of us—me, Bryce, Jake, Nathan, Elijah—we'd all gotten a second chance.

God had been in it this whole time. Even when I couldn't see it. Even when I thought I'd lost everything.

As the sound of laughter and Christmas music

filled the air, as Sophia's giggles rang out among Nathan's rowdy boys, as the firehouse glowed with warmth and love, I knew one thing for certain.

God had brought us all here. He had rewritten every broken story.

Even mine.

I glanced down at Samantha, at the woman who had changed everything for me—who had helped me believe that I wasn't beyond redemption after all.

I lifted her hand to my lips, pressing a kiss against her fingers. And one to where my ring adorned her finger.

She smiled up at me, something knowing in her gaze. "What?"

I shook my head, brushing my thumb over her knuckles. "Just thinking about how much I love you, Mrs. Mercer."

Her breath caught, and for a moment, it was just us—just this woman who had stolen my heart and the future I no longer had to live without.

I cupped her face, letting my fingers trace the curve of her cheek. "I'm so glad I got my second chance with you."

I exhaled, the weight of those words settling deep in my chest. God had been weaving our story together long before either of us had realized it. He had taken everything broken, everything lost, and turned it into something beautiful.

And now? Now, I got to spend forever loving her.

I tipped her chin up and kissed her, slow and reverent, right there in the middle of the party. The sounds of laughter and Christmas music faded as she melted into me, her hands gripping my shirt like she never wanted to let go.

She didn't have to.

Not now. Not ever.

Note to Readers

Thank you for picking up (or downloading!) this book. If you enjoyed it, please consider taking a minute to leave a review or rating! It makes a world of difference for independent authors like myself. I loved writing Samantha and Evan's story. I have to admit - a "secret baby" story was never on my list of favorite story types. I think perhaps the idea of writing characters who had made choices that led to a child out of wedlock was hard for me. But when I chose the title - The One Who Changed Everything - I knew it had to be about a single mom. Nothing has changed my life more than having children!

I loved seeing Evan learn how to accept God's grace for his mistakes - and to forgive himself in the process. And – as for every book in this Second

Chance Fire Station series; the understanding that God's timing is perfect!

I pray my books encourage you in your faith and through your struggles, whatever they may be. I love hearing the amazing ways God has used my words in the lives of my readers. It is incredibly humbling and encouraging! You can email me anytime at tara graceericson@gmail.com.

You can also learn more about my upcoming projects at my website: www.taragraceericson.com or by signing up for my newsletter there. Just for signing up, you'll get two free ebooks and the audio-book of Hawthorne Bloom's story in Hoping for Hawthorne.

Thank you again for all your support and encouragement.

Books by Tara Grace Ericson

Free Stories

Love and Chocolate

Clean Slate (Romantic Suspense)

Black Tower Security

Potential Threat

Hostile Intent

Critical Witness

Imminent Danger

Second Chance Fire Station

The One Who Got Away

The One She Can't Forget

The One Who Promised Forever

The Bloom Sisters Series

Hoping for Hawthorne - A Bloom Family Novella

A Date for Daisy

Poppy's Proposal

Lavender and Lace

Longing for Lily

Resisting Rose

Dancing with Dandelion

Heroes of Freedom Ridge (multi-author series)

Forgiven by the Hero

Believing the Hero (2022 Carol Award Finalist)

Blind Date with the Hero

Seasons of Love Series

Falling on Main Street

Winter Wishes

Spring Fever

Summer to Remember

Kissing in the Kitchen: Series Bonus Novella